W
TWIN
PEAKS

A Complete Guide to
Who's Who & What's What

A P!L **BOOK BY SCOTT KNICKELBINE**

Photo Credits:
© 1990 **Capital Cities/ABC, Inc.**: 11, 15, 19, 21, 24, 28, 58, 62; Cinema Collectors: 22, 34, 36; De Laurentiis Entertainment Group Inc.: 105; © 1990 Entertainment Weekly Inc.: 8; Steve Granitz/Retna Ltd.: 31; Michael Grecco/Outline Press: 32; Ward Keller/World Class Photohistory: 114, 119; © 1990 Karen Kuehn/Matrix: 121; David Lynch/© 1989 Warner Bros. Records: 125; © 1990 Dewey Nicks/Visages: 17; Frank W. Ockenfels/Outline Press: 14; Photofest: 25, 40; The Samuel Goldwyn Company © 1990 PolyGram Filmproduktion GmbH: 106; Siede Preis Photography: 45, 54, 80; © 1990 Craig Sjodin/Capital Cities/ABC, Inc.: 27; *US* Magazine © 1990 Straight Arrow Publishers Inc.: 8; Barry Talesnick/Retna Ltd.: 88; © 1984 Universal City Studios, Inc. and Dino De Laurentiis Corporation: 101; © 1990 Warner Bros., Inc.: 12; © 1990 Warner Home Video: 86.
Front Cover: **Siede Preis Photography**; © 1989 **Leigh A. Rohr**. Other photography by Sam Griffith Studio Inc.

CONTENTS

CHAPTER ONE

AMERICA'S CRAZIEST MYSTERY

All it took was one dead body. One corpse of a homecoming queen, wrapped in plastic and wound in white tape. Its discovery set off an investigation that would slowly, slowly begin to unravel a hundred other mysteries in the little town, a place where everybody seemed so wholesome and decent, but where, in reality, everybody had at least one dirty little secret.

And it took just one corpse in plastic to change the face of television – possibly forever.

The corpse was, of course, the blue and beautiful body of Laura Palmer, and the television show is *Twin Peaks* – the collaboration of David Lynch, one of America's strangest and most critically acclaimed film directors, and Mark Frost, a veteran writer of some of television's most successful shows. *Twin Peaks* had viewers racing home to catch each episode, network execs tearing up their fall scheduling plans, and critics revising their preconceived notions about what's possible on TV.

Most of the television in-group gave *Twin Peaks* about as much chance of survival as a log in a lumberyard. To their chagrin, and to everybody's surprise, the loopy, brooding, and surrealistic soap proved a solid hit with the public. The show topped all shows in the Emmy nominations with 14, beating out such small-screen powerhouses as *L.A. Law, Cheers,* and *Murphy Brown.* Lynch was nominated for producing, directing, writing, creating song lyrics, and composing the series' main title theme music with Angelo Badalamenti. *Twin Peaks* itself was nominated as best drama series, Kyle MacLachlan for best lead actor, Piper Laurie for best lead actress, Sherilyn Fenn for best supporting actress. "I think it's fantastic," Lynch told the *Los Angeles Times.* "I'm going right out to buy a new chain saw and a dozen doughnuts."

The show was also a winner in the ratings game. The April 8, 1990, premiere of *Twin Peaks* got a Nielsen rating of 21.7 and a 33 share, meaning that 33 percent of all those watching television at that time were watching *Twin Peaks.* It ranked number five for the week. The first season's cliff-hanger finale won its time period in the overnight Nielsen ratings.

Robert Iger, president of ABC Entertainment, has said that the survival of the show was never in jeopardy once it stood up respectably to its Thursday night competition, but that many at the network thought the show would fail and fail quickly. But Iger was willing to take a chance: "Once we stop experimenting," he told the *Los Angeles Times,* "once we stop trying to create new viewing experiences, then it's over. Then we're dead."

Originally scoffers, the other networks have taken notice of the phenomenal success of *Twin Peaks.* The presidents of NBC and CBS have both made announcements on programming plans that have widely been interpreted in the industry as allusions to the creative originality of *Twin Peaks.*

Although some of the most important episodes in the first season topped the ratings, the show's survival was in doubt as much of the original audience seemed to slip away. But history suggests that heavy Emmy recognition can stoke a show's ratings, especially a show that needs to "find an audience." One of Mark Frost's previous projects, *Hill Street Blues,* for example, had poor ratings when it first hit the air, but after snagging 21 nominations and virtually sweeping the major awards in 1981, viewership began to grow. It eventually became a ratings success. "I think you can draw a direct comparison to *Hill Street,*" Ted Harbert, ABC's executive vice president for prime time, told the *Los Angeles Times.* "There was a show that started slowly in the ratings and the recognition certainly served as a motivation for people to check it out and see what all the fuss was about."

One thing is for certain: Those who became hooked on the show developed an almost religious fervor about it. All over America, *Peaks* enthusiasts gathered to watch and to celebrate each episode in a way reminiscent of other "cult" television classics such as *Star Trek* and *The Prisoner. Newsweek* magazine noted that "thanks to *Twin Peaks,* trendiness is as simple as turning on the TV each Thursday evening – and then, at work the next day, pretending you understood what the *hell* was going on." The article quotes George Stephanopoulos, assistant to former presidential candidate Dick Gephardt: "Everyone at parties is talking about it. It's gauche to walk away with nothing to say." And Carmen Kroel, San Francisco editor, said, "It's only a TV show, but you feel like a cultural idiot if you can't quote it on Fridays."

Peaks freaks gathered each week to eat cherry pie, sip hot coffee, and watch and discuss each episode. *Twin Peaks* computer networks sprang up, allowing hooked hackers to analyze and dissect the tiniest of details. *Twin Peaks* newsletters, complete with synopses of the latest episodes, began to circulate, and radio stations provided updates the morning after each episode. *Newsweek* published a tongue-in-cheek flow chart that traced the complex relationships among all the characters, living and dead. And the fictional Laura Palmer graced the cover of *Esquire* as the magazine's "Woman of the Year."

Twin Peaks mania struck like a plague. Parents rushed away from a school board meeting in New York State to get to their sets in time for the show. At a Canadian film and television convention, a discussion meant to last until 10:30 Thursday night was abandoned at 8:45 – the conventioneers having returned to their hotel rooms to watch TV. In Los Angeles, a publicist for a new record artist scheduled a showcase performance for early Thursday night and promised the artist would go on at 7:00 sharp so that everyone could be home by 9:00

The evidence of *Twin Peaks*'s popularity was on newsstands all over America – such magazines as *US* and *Entertainment Weekly* carried cover stories on the series.

to watch *Twin Peaks*. At George Washington University, students developed their own Thursday-night pie-eating rituals: The idea is to eat a forkful every time FBI Agent Cooper bites into a slice of cherry or huckleberry.

Pundits were nearly universal in their enthusiasm for the show, which was voted television program of the year by the Television Critics Association. Richard Zoglin of *Time* wrote, "The show has proved that original, challenging and idiosyncratic fare can be done for TV, even within rigid network confines, and that people will tune in."

Howard Rosenberg of the *Los Angeles Times* repeated the theme of much of the critical reaction to *Twin Peaks,* using his admiration for the show as a way of taking a backhanded swipe at the rest of network television. "You're thankful for small pleasures," he wrote. "So much of television is rigidly mainstream as well as simplistic, transparent and without mystique that you almost snap your neck doing a double take when sighting a series as gratuitously bizarre and magnificently opaque as *Twin Peaks.*"

David Ansen in *Newsweek* agreed: "Like a thousand other TV series that it simultaneously emulates, parodies and transcends, *Twin Peaks* uncovers the festering secrets of small-town life. But working firmly within a *Peyton Place* tradition, Lynch performs radical surgery: there

9

is something magically bonkers, and strangely hypnotic, about this show. It mixes naked emotionalism and cool comedy in ways TV viewers aren't accustomed to cope with. Couch potatoes across the land may emerge feeling french-fried." And Ken Tucker in *Entertainment Weekly* wrote, "*Twin Peaks* is different from most other shows that have striven to be innovative, from Larry Gelbart's *United States* to Jay Tarses's *The Days and Nights of Molly Dodd*. For one thing, *Peaks* is *good* – engrossing and funny; for another, it doesn't carry those shows' stink of smugness."

The popularity of *Twin Peaks* has certainly been helped along by one of the most impressive public relations efforts in recent memory. Lynch, normally a reticent kind of guy, was suddenly *everywhere,* giving interviews to *everybody*. The show got prominent play in major magazines as diverse as *Film Comment* and *Glamour,* and even the news shows of competing networks had to stand up and take notice. Rick Kogan, TV critic of the *Chicago Tribune,* noted that the series is "surrounded by as much hype and hoopla as any show I can remember," and that the season premiere was "one of the most anticipated debuts in television history."

Public attention to the show has also been heightened by a push to market *Twin Peaks* products. Ken Scherer, chief operating officer of Lynch/Frost productions, told *The New York Times* that merchandising agreements include a paperback edition of Laura Palmer's diaries, which is being written by Lynch's 22-year-old daughter, Jennifer, and will be published by Simon & Schuster in September 1990. There are also plans to market an audio tape of Agent Dale Cooper's daily instructions to his secretary, Diane. *Twin Peaks* brands of coffee and cherry pie may be available soon in many parts of the country. The requisite T-shirts and coffee mugs may follow, though Frost told *The New York Times,* "David will never approve a conventional T-shirt." Scherer added, "And David said the

Director David Lynch has been elevated to fame with the success of *Twin Peaks*.

The hypnotic, haunting music of *Twin Peaks* has fans flocking to buy Julee Cruise's latest album, which contains "Falling," from the sound track of the show.

JULEE CRUISE
FLOATING INTO THE NIGHT

coffee mug should be shaped like an acorn." Too late about the shirts, though – a man in San Bernardino is already selling T-shirts that say, "I Killed Laura Palmer."

Fans have also been flocking to buy Julee Cruise's album, *Floating into the Night,* a Lynch collaboration with series composer Angelo Badalamenti. "We've had a ton of inquiries about the album," the buyer for a chain of California music stores complained to the *Los Angeles Times.* "We only have one cassette left, but no CDs. That's what everybody wants. . .I heard Warner Bros. just couldn't keep up with the demand."

Where will it all end? No one is certain. *Twin Peaks* has opened up a brand-new area, a sort of Northwest Territory that may be filled with gold mines or hostile Indians. But loyal *Peaks* freaks will be the first to tell you – wherever it ends, they hope it doesn't end soon.

CHAPTER TWO

JUST PLAIN FOLKS

Special Agent Dale Cooper

A rguably the best thing about *Twin Peaks,* Agent Cooper is a straight-arrow FBI agent with a playful, boyish nature and near-psychic deductive powers. Actor Kyle MacLachlan, who plays Cooper, says that Cooper's personality quirks are a combination of traits from David Lynch and Mark Frost. As Michael Sragow has written of Cooper in *American Film,* "MacLachlan puts together combinations of naiveté and authority that would stagger and defeat lesser actors. He catalogues the banal aspects of his mission, like what he eats for lunch on the road (tuna on wheat, slice of cherry pie and coffee), as if the recitation calms him, like a supermundane mantra."

Kyle MacLachlan's career has been tied to Lynch's own. He appeared in Lynch's ill-fated motion picture *Dune* as the messiahlike Paul

Atreides, and he made a big impression on critics in *Blue Velvet* as Jeffrey Beaumont, the all-American boy with a perverted twist. He has appeared in other films as well. MacLachlan made *The Hidden* in 1987 with director Jack Sholden, in which he plays an FBI agent who's actually a space alien. Is it just coincidence that Special Agent Cooper also seems to be (as critic and *Peaks* freak John Leonard puts it) "receiving messages from outer space through fillings in his teeth"?

MacLachlan has been nominated for an Emmy for his role in *Twin Peaks,* and he will also appear in Oliver Stone's soon-to-be-released epic on The Doors.

Left: Kyle MacLachlan, who has appeared in several of Lynch's films, plays the seemingly clairvoyant Agent Cooper. **Opposite:** In *Twin Peaks,* Sheriff Truman (Michael Ontkean) is secretly seeing Josie Packard (Joan Chen).

Sheriff Harry S. Truman

Sheriff Truman is a down-to-earth cop who simply can't fathom Cooper's loopy investigative style. Until the evidence can no longer be denied, he can't believe Cooper's intimations about the dastardly goings-on in Twin Peaks. But he doesn't mind taking a backseat to the brainy FBI agent. "I think I'd better start studying medicine," he tells Cooper, "because I'm beginning to feel like Dr. Watson." Truman is carrying on an affair with Jocelyn Packard, which may prove to be an embarrassment if her secret dealings with Hank Jennings (Norma's husband) ever come to light.

Actor Michael Ontkean, who plays Sheriff Truman, got his first shot at stardom on the TV series *The Rookies*. He has appeared in a number of feature films, including *Slap Shot* and *Maid to Order*. He likes working with MacLachlan: "What you see is an extension of the relationship between Kyle and Michael in real life," he told *Glamour* magazine. "Truman...is a salt-of-the-earth kind of guy. From the outset, he's tickled by this Sherlock Holmes character."

James Hurley

James is a tortured young biker who was secretly seeing Laura Palmer in the weeks before she died. He tried in vain to reform Laura, and now he must avoid the wrath of Laura's two-timing former boyfriend, Bobby Briggs. James is now falling in love with Laura's friend Donna, who warns him that the police are looking for a biker and helps him bury Laura's incriminating necklace. James's father is apparently dead, and his mother seems permanently out of town, so he's looked after by his uncle, Big Ed Hurley. In the season finale, James was being held for possession of the cocaine that Bobby planted in his gas tank.

James Marshall, the 23-year-old actor who plays James, says that in real life he's very much like his brooding character. "I'm very much like my character with women," Marshall told

James Hurley, the lonely boy whose mother is perennially absent, is played by actor James Marshall.

TV Guide. "Innocent, sensitive. The problem is that what a lot of people call sensitive, girls call stupid or naive. I don't have women flocking around me. I don't even have a girlfriend. Women are a complete mystery to me."

Bobby Briggs

Bobby is a nasty piece of work. The smart-mouthed captain of the high school football team, he was the original suspect in Laura's killing. He's carrying on a torrid love affair with Shelly Johnson and at the same time engaging in clandestine drug deals with her brutal husband, Leo. Despite Bobby's bad ways, however, you get the sense that, deep down,

Troublemaker Bobby Briggs is a former boyfriend of Laura Palmer and is the first person suspected by the police of murdering her. Bobby is played by Dana Ashbrook, who also plays a bad-boy part in Bill Cosby's feature *Ghost Dad*.

he's a troubled character. In a scene just before Laura's funeral, we see him before a crucifix: Slowly, he raises his arms to his sides, as if he too is being crucified.

Bobby's bad-boy sexiness has turned actor Dana Ashbrook into a small-screen idol. "I'm really a happy-go-lucky guy, not violent," said Ashbrook, 22, in an interview with the *Los Angeles Times*. "I always felt comfortable around women. I've always been a pretty open, sexual person – I haven't really been too repressed that way." That's fortunate, because the smooch scenes between Bobby and Shelly get hotter than a cup of fresh coffee.

Donna Hayward

Donna, one of Laura's closest friends, is a good-hearted girl who's confused by the mystery and violence surrounding her. She also feels guilty about her feelings for James, Laura's boyfriend. "I should be sad," she confesses to her mother, "but it's like I'm having the most beautiful dream and the most terrible nightmare all at once. I feel like I've betrayed my closest friend. . .but if that's true, why am I so happy?" Donna has joined forces with James, Madeleine (Laura's cousin), and Audrey Horne to solve the riddle of Laura's death.

The actress who plays Donna, 19-year-old Lara Flynn Boyle, is no stranger to television;

Lara Flynn Boyle, who plays Donna Hayward, has also been cast in David Lynch's commercials for Calvin Klein's Obsession fragrance.

she's appeared in *Amerika* and *The Preppie Murder,* as well as several big-screen features. She's an ardent fan of Lynch, and she hopes *Twin Peaks* will continue to be a hit with the fans. "In terms of pace, the ensemble cast and their different personalities, I think definitely they will like it," she told the *Los Angeles Times*. "It's not one of those shows where the 'LAUGH' light goes on, like the sitcoms where you pretty much know when you should laugh and when you should cry."

Pete Martell

Pete is a good old boy who just loves to fish. He's the manager of the Packard Mill, thanks to his marriage to Catherine, sister of the late Andrew Packard. Pete usually seems bewildered and frightened by the events surrounding him, although he does manage to pluck up the nerve to plot with Josie Packard. There's even a hint – just a hint – of a sexual relationship with Josie. But usually, Pete just loves to sit down at the mill, checking off the lumber as it goes by: "Two by fours, four by eights. . .two by fours, four by eights. . .two by fours, four by eights. . ." At the end of the series, we see Pete rush into the burning mill to save Catherine. Will he survive?

Pete is played by Jack Nance, a rubber-faced actor who has appeared in nearly every one of David Lynch's films. Nance met Lynch in Los Angeles in the early '70s and was the unforgettable star of Lynch's *Eraserhead*.

Nance makes a perfect Pete, but he's a little disturbed by his success in the role. He told the *Los Angeles Times,* "I have just been trying to go in and be myself. And I looked at this guy and said, 'God, am I really this weird? Wow, man. Is that really me?'"

Pete Martell, the easygoing mill foreman who found Laura Palmer's body, is played by Jack Nance.

Catherine Martell

Catherine is a bitter woman. She hates Josie Packard, who she feels usurped her position as the natural heir to the Packard Mill. She feels contempt for her husband, Pete, and

21

says, "I know our marriage is a living train wreck." She's even coming to suspect that her lover and co-conspirator, Benjamin Horne, has set her up to be killed in the fire at the Packard Mill. No wonder Catherine seems a little addled sometimes; when she comes upon the screaming, gagged Shelly Johnson at the burning mill, all she can say is, "I can't understand a word you're saying! You have a *thing* in your mouth!"

Catherine is played by Piper Laurie, who has had a distinguished career in films. One of Hollywood's hottest sex symbols in the '50s, she appeared in such movies as *Son of Ali Baba* and *Dawn at Socorro*. In her later career, she tackled more serious roles and won Oscar nominations for her roles in *The Hustler* and *Carrie*. She has also been seen in many television

Josie Packard (Joan Chen, left) and Catherine Martell (Piper Laurie) are in conflict in *Twin Peaks.*

programs, including *In the Matter of Karen Ann Quinlan* and *Tender Is the Night*.

Jocelyn (Josie) Packard

Josie Packard, whom Harry Truman calls "one of the most beautiful women in the state," was discovered by Andrew Packard, the owner of Packard Mills, in Hong Kong. He married her and brought her back to Twin Peaks; when he died a year and a half ago in a boating accident, Josie inherited the whole kit and caboodle.

Josie is a troubled character, and she has a right to be. She's scheming with Pete Martell against his wife Catherine, she's plotting with Benjamin Horne to destroy the mill, and she's made a blood oath with Norma Jennings's husband Hank, who has committed some dastardly crime at her behest. How does she manage to keep all this from her lover, Sheriff Truman?

Joan Chen, who plays Josie, has been a hit with American audiences in such recent movies as *The Last Emperor* and *Tai-Pan,* but the career of this 29-year-old actress actually goes back nearly two decades. As child star Chen Chong, she won the Chinese people's hearts in such blockbusters as *Little Flower* and *Awakening*. She won China's top acting awards before moving to southern California in 1981 to study filmmaking.

Benjamin Horne

Ben Horne is a busy guy; he runs Horne's Department Store and the bordello One-Eyed Jack's, and he is the driving force behind the development of Ghostwood Country Club and Estates. He also finds time to operate a cocaine smuggling ring and plot the destruction of the Packard Mill. Smarmy Benjamin seems to have Twin Peaks wrapped around his little finger – but he can't control his daughter, Audrey. She drives away the Norwegians to whom he was

Benjamin Horne (Richard Beymer) owns just about everything in the town of Twin Peaks.

Richard Beymer (left) and Russ Tamblyn starred together in *West Side Story.* Their paths have crossed since then, and nearly 30 years later they are reunited in *Twin Peaks*.

pitching his country club. Ben sputters, "If you *ever* pull another stunt like that, you're going to be scrubbing bidets in a Bulgarian convent!"

Strangely enough, actor Richard Beymer was originally considered for the role of Dr. Jacoby – a part that eventually went to Beymer's fellow *West Side Story* alumnus, Russ Tamblyn. After meeting Beymer, though, Lynch offered him the role of Benjamin. Although Beymer was a hit as a street tough in *West Side Story,* he's done very few acting roles since, content with producing his own films and experimenting in art.

Audrey Horne

Surely, nobody as sexy as Audrey could possibly be good – and Audrey isn't, although sometimes her intentions are. Her hobbies are spoiling her daddy's plots and spying on everybody. Nevertheless, she "sort of" loved Laura Palmer for working with her disturbed brother Johnny (mental illness "runs in the family," she explains). She goes undercover as a hooker in her father's joint, both to uncover the killer and to help Cooper, whom she obviously finds attractive. She calls him "my special agent."

Audrey is played by Sherilyn Fenn, who won an Emmy nomination as best supporting actress for that role. She has also appeared in several movies, including the 1986 film *The Wraith* and the 1988 film *Two-Moon Junction*.

Big Ed Hurley

Many of the folks in Twin Peaks have to hold down a number of jobs. Ed Hurley not only runs Big Ed's Gas Farm, he's also an undercover agent for the police and a member of the secret society, the Book House Boys. He pines for Norma Jennings, with whom he has had a secret affair, and he tries to cope with the delusions of his one-eyed wife, Nadine. Try as he might, Ed just never seems to please Nadine; when he steps on her drapery runners, she gets so mad she destroys her rowing machine. "It's not the first time, and it won't be the last," Ed confides to Norma afterward, "but I'm in that doghouse again."

Opposite: Sexpot Audrey Horne, daughter of Twin Peaks's biggest businessman, is played by Sherilyn Fenn.
Right: Ed Hurley (Everett McGill) and his obsessed wife, Nadine (Wendy Robie).

Big Ed is played by Everett McGill, an accomplished character actor who often appears in movies and TV playing strong, silent types. David Lynch earlier cast him in the role of the leader of the Fremen warriors in *Dune*.

Norma Jennings

Norma is the tough, yet winsome, owner of the Double R Diner. Although she's in love with Ed Hurley, she nobly breaks up with him to remain true to her husband, Hank, who just got out of prison for manslaughter. On one

Norma Jennings (Peggy Lipton) and Shelly Johnson (Mädchen Amick) both serve up coffee at the Double R Diner.

thing, however, everybody agrees – Norma makes a great huckleberry pie.

Norma is portrayed by Peggy Lipton, who's got to be one of *Twin Peaks*'s most-talked-about comeback stories. If she looks familiar, it's because she played the character of Julie in the '60s TV hit *The Mod Squad*. Since then, however, she's done little work for movies or television. Critics have been pleasantly surprised at the capable way she has handled the role of Norma, who treats nearly everyone she meets with an odd blend of affection and fear.

Shelly Johnson

Shelly is a hard one to figure. She's brutally battered by her husband, Leo, but she stays with him – even though she tries to kill him in one episode. And despite all the turmoil in her life, she remains cheerful in her job behind the counter at the Double R Diner, always having a saucy joke for the patrons. Shelly is, of course, carrying on a torrid illicit affair with Bobby Briggs.

Mädchen Amick, the 19-year-old actress who plays Shelly, says she's not like her part in real life. "I don't know if David does it on purpose, but he tends to cast people as their opposite," Amick told the *San Francisco Chronicle*. "As Shelly, I'm always fighting against my natural instincts. Shelly has to answer to her husband and obey him. But while I was growing up, my parents kept telling me to be my own woman and not let anyone push me around."

Amick has appeared in a number of television productions, including *Baywatch* and *I'm Dangerous Tonight,* and in the feature film *The Boyfriend School.*

Dr. Jacoby

Dr. Jacoby is a cockeyed psychiatrist who normally acts as if he could use a few electroshock treatments himself. He is enamored of things Hawaiian and has filled his house with South Seas images and music. He was secretly treating Laura Palmer, and he found himself falling in love with her. He's deeply at odds with himself. "I'm a terrible person," he confides to Agent Cooper during a midnight encounter over Laura's grave. "I pretend that I'm not, but I am." At the close of the first season, Jacoby is hospitalized. He suffered a heart attack while being attacked as he went to a meeting with Madeleine, who he thinks is Laura.

Jacoby is played by actor Russ Tamblyn, who, with Richard Beymer, made his mark in *West Side Story.* Tamblyn has appeared in many motion pictures, and he won an Oscar nomination for his role in *Peyton Place.* His audition for the role of Dr. Jacoby was so odd

Dr. Jacoby, a psychiatrist who has been treating Laura and who's slightly bonkers himself, is played by actor Russ Tamblyn.

and funny that Lynch decided to give the character more exposure in the series. "David had a different interpretation of [Dr. Jacoby]," Tamblyn said in an interview in *US* magazine. "He was supposed to be seedy and sleazy. I just decided to make him eccentric as hell."

The Log Lady

Everybody calls her the Log Lady because she carries around a log with secret knowledge. "Can I ask her about the log?" Cooper asks Truman. "Many have," Harry replies. The Log Lady says mysteriously, "One day, my log will have something to say about this. My log saw something that night. . ."

The character of the Log Lady, played by Catherine Coulson, is certainly the most obscure, and perhaps the best loved, in *Twin Peaks*. Strange as it may seem, Lynch foresaw the role nearly 20 years ago, when he cast Coulson as one of Henry's neighbors in *Eraserhead*. "I had an idea for a show," Lynch told *Rolling Stone*. "I wanted to call it 'I'll Test My Log With Every Branch of Knowledge.' And I

The bizarre character of the Log Lady, who cradles her all-knowing log in her arms, is played by Catherine Coulson.

wanted her to be a woman who lived with a son or daughter, single, because her husband was killed in a fire. She takes the log to various experts in various fields of science. . .So through the log, through this kind of absurdity, you would learn, you'd be gaining so much knowledge through the show. So when it came to shoot the *Twin Peaks* pilot, I called Catherine."

Laura Palmer

Who was Laura Palmer, really? Was she the popular, do-gooding high school girl, organizing meals-on-wheels programs and tutoring the handicapped? Or was she the wild child, the coke sniffer, the secretive nymphomaniac with a thing for bondage and a passion for murderous sex? Actually, all we know of Laura is a collection of other people's recollections, from boyfriend James's loving memories to Jacques Renault's smutty stories of sex parties in his forest cabin. The real mystery of *Twin Peaks* may not be so much the identity of Laura Palmer's killer as it is the true identity of Laura Palmer herself.

Sheryl Lee, the 23-year-old Chicago native who plays Laura Palmer – and her look-alike cousin, Madeleine – has received enormous attention for the role. She appeared on the cover of *Esquire* – wrapped, appropriately enough, in plastic – when the magazine named

Was Laura Palmer the all-American, wholesome homecoming queen – or was she the force that dragged others into evil?

Laura Palmer their "Woman of the Year." Lynch has capitalized on her fame by casting her as the Good Witch of the West in the climax of his latest film, *Wild at Heart*.

Sheryl is remaining tight-lipped about the identity of her character's killer – if she even knows. "Someone even suggested Laura committed suicide," Lee said in an interview with Scripps-Howard News Service. "Does this mean I killed myself and wrapped myself in plastic?"

CHAPTER THREE

"IT'S LIKE A BEAUTIFUL DREAM. . .AND THE MOST TERRIBLE NIGHTMARE"

Episode One

T his two-hour series pilot was directed by David Lynch.

In the bucolic Northwest lumber town of Twin Peaks, Pete Martell discovers a body on the riverfront outside the Packard Mill. He calls Sheriff Truman. . ."She's dead, wrapped in plastic," he sputters. Truman, Deputy Andy, and Doc Hayward go to inspect the body, which they discover to be that of Laura Palmer – the most popular girl in town. The body is wrapped in plastic sheeting and wound in white tape.

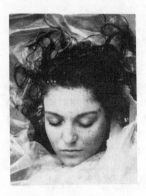

Twin Peaks begins with the discovery of Laura Palmer's body wrapped in plastic.

Meanwhile, Mrs. Palmer calls frantically around town, trying to find the missing Laura. Her husband, Leland, is at the Great Northern Hotel with Benjamin Horne making a sales pitch for "Ghostwood Country Club and Estates" to a group of Norwegians. It becomes apparent that Horne hasn't yet acquired the land for the development. Leland is called out of the presentation to answer a phone call from his wife. At that moment, Truman drives up to inform Leland of his daughter's death. This scene – with the Sheriff wordlessly conveying the tragic news, and an extended shot of the dropped telephone receiver, over which we hear Mrs. Palmer screaming – is one of the most powerful in the series. It's also unusual for a television whodunit. Usually, the discovery of a corpse is simply the event that gets the investigation underway; here, it is treated sensitively, like something happening to real human beings.

Next we are introduced to the Double R Diner and its owner, Norma Jennings. Bobby Briggs, Laura's boyfriend, is there and offers Shelly Johnson, the waitress, a ride home. Bobby and Shelly are having a secret affair. Shelly assures Bobby that her husband, Leo, is not at home – he called her from Butte, Montana, at midnight and couldn't possibly be back yet. But as Bobby drives toward Shelly's house, Leo's truck – an ominous, powerful-looking truck – is in front of the house.

At the high school, Donna Hayward and James Hurley, two of Laura's closest friends, are shocked at the announcement of Laura's death. Bobby is called in for questioning and denies killing Laura. The school principal makes a tearful announcement over the intercom system, and the camera slowly moves in to a portrait of Laura in the school's trophy case. The clear implication is that the town has lost one of its finest young girls, someone that everyone loved. But we learn later that there is more than one side to Laura Palmer.

Under sedation, Mrs. Palmer tells the police that she last saw Laura go into her room at 9:00 the previous evening, where she apparently received one phone call. In Laura's bedroom, the police find her diary, which is locked, and a video camera. Word comes that Mr. Pulaski, one of the workers at the mill, has reported that his daughter has been missing since last night.

Josie Packard, a beautiful Chinese woman who is the widow of the mill's owner, Andrew Packard, was glimpsed at the beginning of the episode, but she is more thoroughly introduced at a scene at the sawmill. She is in conflict with Catherine Martell, Andrew's sister and the mill's manager, over whether to close the mill for the day. Josie exercises her will, and the mill is closed. Then we see Ronette Pulaski, walking zombielike over a railroad trestle, half-naked, bloody, and still bound at the wrists.

Was Ronette Pulaski – wounded and dazed, but still alive – another victim of Laura's murderer?

FBI Special Agent Dale Cooper drives into town, primly dressed in a dark suit and tie and dictating the minutiae of his travels to his secretary, Diane, into a microcassette recorder. When he meets Sheriff Truman – Harry S. Truman, that is – he immediately questions Truman about the local trees, beginning his preoccupation with the local flora and fauna.

The first stop for Cooper and Harry is the hospital, where they visit Ronette Pulaski. "Don't go there, don't go there!" Ronette mutters in her coma.

As Cooper and Harry head down to the morgue, we glimpse a one-armed man who gets out of the elevator before them. He is on the screen just long enough for us to realize he will be important. Next, a slightly bonkers, grey-bearded man introduces himself as Dr. Jacoby, a psychiatrist. Pulling away one of the huge cotton swabs he has stuck in his ears, Jacoby explains that Laura was one of his patients, but that Laura's parents didn't know it.

Cooper inspects the body of Laura Palmer. The fluorescent lights flicker, creating a weird, grisly atmosphere. Under the nail of her ring finger, he finds a tiny scrap of paper with the letter R on it. "Diane! It's the same thing!" Cooper yells into his recorder, which he's set on the corpse's belly for the purpose. In fact, he was looking for something under Ronette Pulaski's fingernail, but he didn't find it. He

For some reason, Agent Cooper expects to find a clue under Laura's fingernail – and he does.

doesn't explain *what* the same thing is. Then he beams at Sheriff Truman: "We have a lot to talk about."

Back at the station house, Cooper springs open Laura's diary and finds two significant entries (which he is careful to record for Diane): the last, dated February 23, which reads "Nervous about meeting J tonight," and one 18 days earlier, which includes an envelope containing a safety deposit box key and white powder, and reads simply, "Day One." Cooper speculates that the white powder is cocaine, but Harry can't believe it. Laura?

Armed with Laura's mysterious videotape, Cooper questions suspects Bobby and Donna about a scene in the tape that shows Laura and

Donna cavorting at a picnic. This is our first view of the murdered girl alive. As she brings her face close to the camera, we see a blonde girl with a knowing smile. The scene on the tape ends with a close-up of Laura's eye. The reflection of a motorcycle's headlights can be seen in her eye.

Audrey, Benjamin Horne's sexy daughter who is also in school with Bobby, James, and Donna, plays one of her mischievous tricks. She frightens the Norwegians with tales of Laura's death, and they leave the hotel without closing the deal.

Cooper and Harry Truman go to an abandoned rail car, which appears to be the place where Laura and Ronette were tortured. They find a strange mound of dirt, and on top of it is a necklace with half of a golden heart dangling from it. Nearby is a scrap of paper on which is written – apparently in blood – the cryptic message, "Fire walk with me." Next, we see James Hurley, his motorbike by his side, sitting and looking out toward the mountains. He is holding the other half of the heart.

Later, in Laura's safety deposit box, Cooper discovers $10,000 in cash and a copy of *Flesh World* magazine. In the magazine, he finds personal ads from Ronette Pulaski and Leo Johnson – Leo's ad featuring a photo of his truck identical to the shot of his truck in the scene with Bobby and Shelly.

Speaking of Leo Johnson, the next scene illustrates his villainous possessiveness of his wife, Shelly. He has discovered different brands of cigarettes in the ashtray, and he warns her that she had better behave like a model wife.

That night a town meeting is called. Sheriff Truman points out to Cooper several of the town's leading citizens, including Benjamin Horne, who "owns half of Twin Peaks," Josie Packard, widow of Andrew Packard and heiress to his sawmill, and a weird lady carrying a log as if it were a baby. Everybody calls her "the Log Lady." Cooper tells the assembled townsfolk that the murder of Laura Palmer resembles another that occurred almost exactly a year ago in another part of the state. "There is a chance that the person who committed these crimes is someone from this town, possibly even someone you know," he tells them.

Donna overhears her father, Dr. Hayward, telling her mother about the heart necklace, so she sneaks out of the house to go to the Road House to warn James Hurley that Cooper is looking for a biker. James was secretly seeing Laura in the weeks before her death.

Julee Cruise appears as the lead singer with the band at the Road House, performing "Falling" and "The Nightingale" – which, pretty as they might be, don't strike one as the sort of numbers that would appeal to the patrons of the bar. The scene is crowded with people connected with Laura. Bobby Briggs is there with Donna's jealous boyfriend, Mike. Big Ed Hurley – James's uncle and the owner of Big Ed's Gas Farm – is there, having a rendezvous with his secret love, Norma Jennings. When Donna walks in, a fight breaks out as Mike confronts her and Big Ed tries to protect her.

Donna slips away with another biker, who takes her to the forest to meet James. Laura was with James the night she died. "Donna, she was a different person," James says – a remark that foreshadows the confusion over Laura's identity as the series continues. James says that Laura said something about a guy getting killed. "Bobby told her that he killed this guy," he says. "It all makes some kind of terrible sense that she died." Now, Donna and James discover they are in love. They decide to bury the incriminating necklace. As they leave on James's motorbike, James is arrested – Agent Cooper and Sheriff Truman have been tailing them all along. James is taken to jail, where Mike and Bobby are already locked up.

Cooper's next preoccupation is getting a hotel room – "a clean place, reasonably priced" is what he wants, and Harry promises to get him a good rate at the Great Northern. Happily, Cooper dictates the news to Diane on his way out of the sheriff's station.

Truman has a midnight rendezvous with Josie Packard, with whom he is obviously having an affair. "It must have happened about this time," he muses, staring out at the dark waterfront. Meanwhile, Mrs. Palmer has a vision of a gloved hand digging up the heart necklace and starts to scream.

Episode Two

A slow pan travels over the details of Agent Cooper's room in the Great Northern as we hear him recounting the room's good points to Diane. Then we see Cooper – hanging by his feet from a rod. (Lynch fans will note that this is exactly the posture in which we first glimpse Henry in *Eraserhead*. Was the episode's director, Duwayne Dunham, paying a clever tribute to Lynch?) In the hotel's coffee shop, Cooper gives the hotel his final seal of approval when he is served "a *damn* fine cup of coffee."

At the sheriff's station, after consuming enormous bitefuls of doughnuts from a huge buffet of them, Cooper and Truman go over the autopsy report on Laura Palmer. Dr. Hayward says the cause of death was loss of blood from numerous shallow wounds and bite marks – and that the victim had had sex with at least three different men before she died. Time of death was between midnight and 4:00 A.M. Meanwhile, Shelly Johnson discovers a blood-soaked shirt in husband Leo's laundry, and she hides it away.

Shelly finds blood on her husband's shirt – is Leo
Johnson guilty of Laura's murder?

James confesses to Cooper and Truman
that he shot the mysterious video. He tells the
officers that Laura resumed her cocaine habit a
couple of days ago, because "something
happened. . .something scared her." He admits
being with Laura the night she died. He says
that Laura met him around 9:30, and she rode
with him on his motorbike. But at 12:30, at the
traffic light at the corner of Sparkwood and 21,
she jumped off and ran away into the night. He
doesn't tell them that she gave him the other
half of the heart on the day marked "Day One"
in her diary, but as he plays the scene over again
in his mind, we see his vision of Laura, happy
because she knows James loves her.

45

Leo Johnson gets upset when he can't find his bloody shirt – a clue that seems to implicate him as the killer. Back at the jail, Bobby and Mike explain their connection with a cocaine ring. Because Laura was supposed to provide the $10,000 for the second payment to Leo Johnson, and the money is still in her safe deposit box, they can't complete their cocaine deal with Leo.

We see another glimpse of the video of Laura – and as her face fills the frame, through the music, we hear a ghostly voice saying, "Help me."

Big Ed Hurley, who was actually on a stakeout at the Road House the night before, comes to the station to pick up James. He says he thinks his beer was drugged by the proprietor, Jacques Renault. After James is released into Ed's custody, he tells Ed that he'll need a hand from the Book House Boys to cover his back. At this point, we know nothing about the Book House Boys – that's explained in a later episode, and when it is explained, it's surprising and illuminating that James is involved.

Bobby and Mike are also released from jail, since the charge against them was merely disorderly conduct arising from the fight at the Road House.

The sheriff and Cooper go to see Josie Packard. Pete Martell, who is with her, pours out coffee, which is always welcome to Agent

Cooper. He likes it "black as midnight on a moonless night."

Josie says Laura was tutoring her in English and that she last saw Laura the previous Thursday afternoon for a lesson. "Something was bothering her. . .she said, 'I think now I understand how you feel about your husband's death.'"

When Josie leaves the room, Agent Cooper asks, "So, Harry, how long have you been seeing her?" Nonplussed, Harry asks, "How did you know?" "Body language," Cooper replies. Harry then explains to Cooper that Andrew Packard died a year and a half ago in a boating accident. Just as Cooper and Harry raise their cups to their lips, Pete rushes in and urges, "Don't drink the coffee! There was a fish in the percolator."

Ben Horne and Catherine Martell – another illicit couple – are seen having a post-coital strategy session about gaining control of the mill. "A few more local tragedies, and Josie might just run the old mill into the ground all by herself," Ben says. But Catherine is impatient. "Maybe it's time to start a little fire," Ben says.

During a touching visit from Donna, Mrs. Palmer has a frightening vision of a long-haired man. At this point, it looks as if Mrs. Palmer is going to crack under the strain before Leland Palmer, but later in the series it turns out that the opposite is true.

We learn that Ronette Pulaski worked at the perfume counter at Horne's Department Store before her murder. And Deputy Hawk discovers a one-armed man lurking around the morgue.

A brief, kooky glance at Bobby Briggs's home life shows Major Briggs trying to establish "meaningful dialogue" to bring Bobby out of his indolent shell. He reassures Bobby in an officious, military way that "rebellion is expected in a boy your age." But when Bobby sticks a cigarette in his mouth, the Major strikes him so hard that the butt goes flying – right into Mrs. Briggs's food. The Major begins droning on again, as if nothing had happened.

Cooper and Truman go to the Double R Diner, where the special agent wolfs three pieces of pie. "You must have the metabolism of a bumble bee!" Harry exclaims. Cooper meets the Log Lady, who says, "One day, my log will have something to say about this. My log saw something that night."

Leo Johnson, who has been cutting open a football, hears Shelly coming home. Carefully he prepares a weapon: a bar of soap fitted into a sock. Confronting her about the missing shirt, he starts to beat her, twirling his sock over his head. She collapses against the plastic sheeting over an unfinished wall.

In the privacy of his Hawaiian-decor office, Dr. Jacoby listens to a tape of Laura talking about a "mystery man," and we discover that Jacoby has hidden the other half of the heart necklace in a coconut. As Jacoby listens through his headphones and dangles the necklace in front of him, his eyebrows shoot up in surprise, and he begins to weep. Wait a minute. . .maybe *Jacoby* is the killer!

Episode Three

This is the second episode directed by David Lynch, and his slow, mysterious directorial style drips down every scene like syrup off a stack of hotcakes.

Benjamin Horne's brother Jerry introduces Benjamin to the joys of brie-and-baguette sandwiches. Ben tells his brother about Laura's death and the departure of the Norwegians. To cheer him up, Ben tells him about a new girl at One-Eyed Jack's – "freshly scented from the perfume counter." The two race off in a long, elegant motorboat to One-Eyed Jack's – a bordello and casino in the forest, just over the Canadian border. The midnight meeting at One-Eyed Jack's, with its slow pacing, its low lighting, saturated in amber, and the mysterious, symmetrical presentation of the prostitutes, creates a sense of mystery and evil.

Deputy Hawk finds a one-armed man in intensive care at the hospital, and Cooper returns to his room at the Great Northern to find under his door a perfumed note reading "Jack with One Eye."

In the woods, Bobby and Mike discover a hollowed-out football, but not all of the cocaine they ordered is in it. Leo comes to yell at them because Bobby hasn't got the rest of the money. "Leo needs a new pair of shoes," he insists. He also hints that he's on to Bobby and Shelly's affair. A shadowy figure lurks in the background.

At the Hurleys' house, Big Ed manages to drip grease on his wife Nadine's drape runners. Nadine's obsession with perfectly silent drape runners is a continuing theme in the series.

The next morning, Cooper assembles Truman, Lucy (the receptionist at the sheriff's department), and Truman's associates Andy and Hawk at a blackboard outdoors. Agent Cooper, in one of his pedantic little speeches, outlines a particularly off-the-wall approach to detective work. After a brief lecture on Tibet (complete with map on the reverse side of the blackboard), he says that after a dream he had three years ago, he realized he had "subconsciously gained knowledge of a deductive technique involving mind-body coordination operating hand in hand with the deepest level of intuition." This might be the explanation of Cooper's Holmesian ability to come up with observations that seem to be psychic. The present use of the technique involves chucking rocks at a milk bottle while Truman recites the names of suspects whose names contain the letter J. The scene is actually quite helpful to viewers who are still confused about which character is which, because as Truman calls out the name, the face of the suspect appears on the screen. Cooper throws his rocks, hitting the bottle when Dr. Jacoby's name is read and smashing the bottle when Truman calls out the name of Leo Johnson. Does this mean Leo Johnson is the killer? The group reflects solemnly, surrounded by doughnuts and logs.

Donna and Audrey meet at the Double R Diner. "Did Laura ever talk about my father?" Audrey asks, but she refuses to elaborate. At the end of the scene, Audrey does her controlled, yet sensuous, dance to Badalamenti's music, which is playing on the jukebox.

Forensic pathologist Albert Rosenfield, whom Cooper describes as having limited social skills, arrives from Washington and insults Lucy and Harry mercilessly. Nadine tells Big Ed she's finally developed a perfectly silent drape runner, thanks to Ed's having spilled oil on it. Pete Martell gives Josie the key to Catherine's wall safe, where she discovers two separate accounting ledgers for the mill.

Leland Palmer, Laura's father, has his own dance – with Laura's photograph, while he plays a record of the Glenn Miller song "Pennsylvania 6-5000." It's a bizarre scene, in which he says over and over, "We have to dance for Laura –

dance for Laura." At last, in a struggle with his wife, the glass over the photograph smashes. Leland cuts his hand, smearing blood over the face of Laura in the photograph. The poignant music swells, reminding us of the grief of first hearing of Laura's death.

That night, back at the Great Northern, Agent Cooper has a dream. Because Cooper himself believes the dream to hold the solution to Laura's murder – and because the sequence is one of the wildest things ever to be shown on network television – we'll describe it in detail:

A voice in the distance calls "Laura." We see flashing images of Cooper as an older man, of the back of a dwarf, of Mrs. Palmer running down the stairs, of the long-haired man of Mrs. Palmer's vision, of a bloody cloth, and Laura's face on the autopsy table.

Then we see the one-armed man, who recites: "In the darkness of future past/The Magician longs to see/One chance heart between two worlds/Fire, walk with me."

"We lived among the people," the one-armed man continues. "How do you say. . . convenience store. We lived above it. I mean it like it is. . .and it sounds. I too have been touched by the devilish one. A tattoo on the left shoulder. Ah, but when I saw the face of God, I was changed. I took the entire arm off." He smiles. "My name is Mike. His name is Bob." We see a vision of Bobby, lying face down.

Just then, the long-haired man calls "Mike! Mike! Can you hear me?" Then he turns to us and says, "Catch you with my death bag! You may think I have gone insane, but I promise I will kill again." A circle of candles is blown out.

Now Cooper – the older Cooper – is seated in a chair, looking at the back of the dwarf while the sound of rubbing palms – or flapping wings – fills the air. Cooper looks over at a sofa, where Laura Palmer is seated. The dwarf turns around, rubs his hands, and says, "Let's rock!" The camera moves back to show us a room surrounded in red curtains, with a black love seat and sofa, two trumpetlike lamps, and a Grecian-style statue of a woman whose arms conceal her breasts and thighs.

The strangeness of the scene is heightened by the weird way the dwarf and the woman speak and move. The actors originally performed their roles backward – walking backward, reading their lines backward. The result, when reversed, is strange and nightmarish. Fortunately, subtitles help us to understand what they're saying.

Slowly, Laura places a finger alongside her nose. The shadow of a bird – or possibly a person walking – passes over the curtains. "I've got good news," says the dwarf. "That gum you like is going to come back in style." He looks at Laura. "She's my cousin. But doesn't she look almost exactly like Laura Palmer?"

I feel like I know her, but
sometimes my arms bend back.

Like all dreams, Agent Cooper's is full of obscure
references, but he thinks it holds the key to the mystery.

"But it is Laura Palmer," Cooper says. "Are
you Laura Palmer?"

"I feel like I know her, but sometimes my
arms bend back," is the woman's enigmatic
reply.

"She's filled with secrets," the dwarf goes
on. "Where we're from, the birds sing a pretty
song, and there's always music in the air."
Swanky music starts playing, lights start flashing
– reminding us of the flashing lights in the
morgue – and the dwarf begins to dance. Laura
comes over and plants a kiss on Cooper and
begins to whisper teasingly in his ear.

Cooper awakes from his dream, and still
hearing the music and snapping his fingers,

calls Truman. He announces, "I know who killed Laura Palmer." We think we know, too – forget Leo Johnson! The killer is Bob, the long-haired man!

Episode Four

Scheming little Audrey, who appears to be developing an interest in Cooper, meets him at breakfast and admits writing the note under his door that said, "Jack with One Eye." One-Eyed Jack's, she explains, is a place just across the Canadian border where girls work. She says she doesn't know if Laura worked at One-Eyed Jack's, but she did work at the perfume counter at Horne's Department Store.

When Lucy and Sheriff Truman arrive, Cooper gives them a slightly different version of his dream than the one we saw. Placidly, he continues to tell his dream, disregarding their – and our – eagerness to know who killed Laura Palmer. He says that the woman in the dream whispered it in his ear – but he can't remember who it was. However, he insists, "My dream is a code, waiting to be broken. Break the code, solve the crime."

Albert, the forensic pathologist, has a fight in the autopsy room with Dr. Hayward and Truman. Albert wants to delay the funeral so he can eviscerate Laura's body, but the townspeople protest. Finally, Harry lands a haymaker on Albert that sends him sprawling across the corpse. Cooper intervenes on behalf of the family – a sign that his sympathies may be leaning more toward the folks at Twin Peaks than they do to his bureaucratic employers in Washington. In fact, he later dictates another note to Diane – these notes become less frequent the longer Cooper stays in Twin Peaks – saying, "I'd like you to look into my pension plan options regarding outside real estate investment. I may look into purchasing a piece of property at what I may assume will be a very reasonable price." What can he mean? Is he planning to settle in Twin Peaks? Or is he, too, interested in the sawmill property?

Before Laura's funeral, a despondent Leland Palmer is watching the soap opera that everyone in Twin Peaks follows, *Invitation to Love*. In the episode, a man who is apparently intending to commit suicide says, "My darling daughter, Jade…" At that moment, the doorbell rings, and Laura's cousin Madeleine arrives to comfort him. She looks startlingly like Laura – a Laura wearing glasses, and with brown hair instead of blonde. A voice in the soap opera says, "Surprised?"

Norma discusses with a prison official the parole of her husband Hank, who's doing three to five for vehicular manslaughter. Cooper and the Sheriff go to see Leo Johnson. While he continues to cut wood up with an axe – this axe will have a more gruesome purpose later – he says he has the perfect alibi: On the night of Laura's murder, he was in Butte, Montana.

Back at the station, Albert disdainfully goes over his findings with Cooper. Laura had a cocaine habit, Albert reveals. Before her death she had been bound twice, once with her elbows high up. "Sometimes my arms bend back," Cooper mutters. The wounds on Laura's shoulder were bite and claw marks from some animal. In Laura's stomach was a fragment of plastic with the letter J on it – bringing our thoughts back to the letter J in her diary and the letter R under her fingernail. What does it mean?

At Laura's funeral, all hell breaks loose. Bobby calls the assembled mourners "hypocrites." "You want to know who killed Laura," he says. "We all did." Leland Palmer loses control altogether and dives onto the coffin, which begins to move up and down in the grave, accompanied by an eerie mechanical sound. Mrs. Palmer wails, "Don't ruin this, too!"

The entire funeral sequence is similar to other scenes in *Twin Peaks* – the baguette-eating scene, or the scene where Leland freaks out at the Icelandic gala – in which order and repose suddenly seem to give way to madness and chaos. It is a theme that appears frequently in Lynch's films, as well: think of Henry's dinner

Shelly, Norma, Ed and Nadine, and Agent Cooper stand at the graveside during Laura's funeral.

with Mary X. in *Eraserhead,* or the scene in which a naked, bleeding Dorothy stumbles into the well-kept living room of Jeffrey's girlfriend in *Blue Velvet.* Insanity, Lynch seems to suggest, lies just under the surface of normality.

Back at the Double R Diner, Cooper joins Truman, Big Ed, and Hawk, and orders himself a slice of huckleberry pie, heated, with vanilla ice cream on the side and, of course, coffee. He also performs another one of his instantaneous deductions: "Big Ed, how long have you been in love with Norma?"

Harry Truman tells Cooper that they know someone has been running drugs into Twin

Peaks from across the border. They've targeted Jacques Renault, the bartender at the Road House, as the middleman. Harry reveals that Ed is working undercover on this.

"Twin Peaks is different – a long way from the world," Harry says. "You've noticed that." He describes an evil in the woods, a dark presence that has been out there a long time and that takes many forms. A secret society called the Book House Boys has banded together to fight the evil in the forest. The sign of this secret society seems to be laying a finger on the forehead, beside the eyes. The four go to the Book House, where Bernard Renault, the brother of Jacques from the Road House, is tied up. They suspect Bernard of being involved in the ring with his brother. Bernard provides no answers. Meanwhile, Jacques, on his way to the Road House, sees a flashing light – a signal that his brother is in trouble. He phones Leo Johnson, and Leo goes to meet him.

Shelly Johnson has provided herself with a gun – presumably for protection against her brutal husband. At the mill, Josie Packard tells Harry about the two ledgers, but when she opens the safe, one of them has disappeared. "Something horrible is going to happen," Josie says. We see Catherine Martell hiding the second ledger in her desk. Cooper finds Dr. Jacoby at Laura's grave, and the psychiatrist admits his love for Laura.

Episode Five

From this point on in the series, things begin to move very quickly, and *Twin Peaks* loses a bit of its dreamy pacing. Mark Frost, who wrote this and the last episode without Lynch, said in an interview with *The New York Times,* "Generally my internal pace is faster than David's. But the episodes I wrote alone are building to a climax in the story, so it's hard to know if that's really my pace or a reaction to what's happening in the plot."

Mrs. Palmer reveals to the police that she's had a vision of a long-haired man crouching at the foot of Laura's bed. She also tells of the vision she had exactly 24 hours after Laura's death – that of the gloved hand digging up a necklace. Donna Hayward realizes she's describing James's half of the necklace.

Did someone say necklace? In the very next scene, we're staring at a necklace that bounces on the bosom of Emerald, a character in *Invitation to Love.* Lucy's watching the show at the sheriff's office. Truman asks Lucy, "What's happening?" She begins to describe the convoluted tale of the soap opera, filled with romance, intrigue, and far too many characters to keep track of. What could that remind us of?

Jacoby is at the sheriff's office, sitting in front of the map of Tibet, wearing glasses with one red lens and one blue lens, and doing magic tricks. Cooper questions him about Laura's problems, but the psychiatrist is evasive. "Laura had secrets, and around those secrets she built a fortress." He tells Cooper that the night after Laura's death, he followed a man in a red Corvette, but lost him on the old mill road. Jacoby leaves, and we get a few more clues: Cooper confirms that a police sketch of the man in Mrs. Palmer's vision was the same long-haired man that was in his dream. We learn that Leo Johnson has a red Corvette. FBI forensics phones up and says that the wounds on Laura's body were bird bites. And Hawk has found the one-armed man staying at the Timber Falls Motel.

Guess who else is at the seedy motel? Benjamin and Catherine, having another post-boff strategy meeting. Catherine is anxious to burn down the mill, and Ben assures her that the headlines will read "Josie Packard Torches Bankrupt Mill in Insurance Fraud." Something falls out of his pocket. Catherine picks it up – it's a poker chip from One-Eyed Jack's. Little do both of them suspect that Josie is in her car outside, spying on them.

The cops arrive and – after a tense moment during which Andy drops his gun, which goes off – break into the motel room of the one-armed man. He turns out to be a harmless-looking shoe salesman named Mr. Gerard – his

Catherine Martell and Benjamin Horne have their own ideas about the future of the Packard Mill.

middle name is Michael – who's been at the hospital to visit a sick friend, the veterinarian Bob Lydecker. Aha! Mike and Bob? But when confronted with the sketch of the long-haired man, Gerard denies ever having seen him before. He lost the arm in a car accident – and the tattoo on his arm didn't read, "Fire walk with me" – it said, "Mom." Outside the hotel room, Hawk identifies Josie's car track in the sand, so that Sheriff Truman knows that she was there.

Back at the high school, Audrey and Donna have a little tête-à-tête in the ladies' room. Audrey tells Donna she's been "doing some research" – primarily to get Agent Cooper's attention. She's learned that Laura was secretly a patient of Jacoby. She knows that Laura and Ronette both worked at the perfume counter at Horne's Department Store, and she suspects Laura worked as a hooker at One-Eyed Jack's. "That would sure explain a few things," Donna replies. Donna agrees to cooperate with Audrey in her undercover work – as long as she agrees to keep it secret between themselves.

Norma goes to Hank's parole hearing. Hank protests to the board that he's a victim of fate: "A car in perfect condition goes out of control," he says of the event that landed him in the pokey. "A vagrant nobody knows is killed sleeping by the roadside." Norma assures the prison officials she'll give Hank a job, while all the while the con fingers a domino piece.

Truman and Cooper visit the local "One-Stop" – the convenience store in Cooper's dream? – and, lo and behold, there is the Lydecker veterinary practice right across the street! The office is crowded with strange animals; Cooper pauses to stare down a llama. Cooper is certain the bird who made the marks on Laura's shoulder was a patient of Lydecker's, so he confiscates their records.

Bobby and Shelly have a steamy love scene, during which Shelly tells him her husband Leo's been hanging out with Jacques Renault. She shows him Leo's bloody shirt, and we can see Bobby's wheels turning. "Leo's not going to be a problem for us any more," he tells her.

Cooper, Truman, Hawk, and Andy decide to do a little target practice at the pistol range while Lucy goes through the veterinarian's records. Andy's mystified that Lucy has been so cold to him lately. We get a rare glimpse into Cooper's love life. "I knew someone once who helped me understand commitment, the responsibility and the risks. . .who taught me the pain of a broken heart," he says, and then blows four holes in his target with his pistol – two bullets through each eye, and one through each nostril.

Meanwhile, at the Double R Diner, Shelly and Norma are commiserating about *their* troubles with men. "Two men apiece, and we don't know what to do with any of the four of them," Norma sighs. "I've definitely got plans for Leo," Shelly replies darkly. A few minutes later, Norma gets a phone call telling her that her husband, Hank, has been paroled.

Madeleine, Laura's look-alike cousin, walks into the diner, and James is shocked to see her. He introduces himself, and Maddy tells him she's from Missoula, Montana (incidentally, that's David Lynch's home town), and that she and Laura used to pretend they were sisters as children.

Back at the Great Northern, Audrey beguiles her father into giving her a job at Horne's Department Store. Ben gets a mysterious call and sets up a meeting at the river.

The boys back at the FBI phone Cooper to say that they've reconstructed the object in Laura Palmer's stomach – it's a poker chip. And we learn that one of Lydecker's patients was a mynah bird named Waldo. . .owned by none other than Jacques Renault. They race to Renault's apartment and find Leo Johnson's bloody shirt, which has just been planted there by Bobby.

At the river, Ben meets – Leo Johnson! Leo has just killed Bernard Renault to keep him from spilling the beans on his coke business, which it turns out Ben is involved in. Ben wants Leo to torch the Packard Mill. "Keep it simple," he says, "The insurance investigator should read 'ARSON' in block letters about six feet high."

In the forest, James and Donna confirm their fears that the heart they buried is missing. Josie gets a call from Truman, who asks her why she was at the motel that morning, but she is evasive. Pete Martell gets Josie to agree to join him in a mixed-doubles fishing tournament. Then the Widow Packard gets a more menacing proposition: a picture of a domino in the mail, and a threatening phone call from Hank Jennings.

Episode Six

Agent Cooper is jolted from his sleep by the carousing of a group of Icelanders, whom

Jerry Horne has brought to Twin Peaks to finance Ghostwood. Early the next morning, he stumbles down for breakfast – clutching his coffee mug, which bears the seal of the Federal Bureau of Investigation.

Benjamin Horne is also leery about the Icelanders. His plans for a gala reception for the visitors are cut short by a distraught Leland Palmer, who tries to get involved once more in Ben's affairs. Poor Leland breaks down in hysterics.

Cooper, Truman, Andy, and Dr. Hayward continue their investigation at Jacques Renault's apartment. Cooper has a hunch that the blood on Leo's shirt is Jacques' – a premonition that turns out to be correct.

Andy goes to the Johnson residence to find Leo, and Shelly (who's been coached by Bobby) makes some incriminating remarks about her husband's transactions with Jacques Renault. At Big Ed's Gas Farm, Ed tells Norma he can't leave Nadine, so Norma bravely breaks off her affair with him. Audrey pressures the manager at Horne's to give her a job at the perfume counter, though he protests it's a "sensitive position."

James reveals to Donna that his father isn't really dead – he just ran off; his mother, an alcoholic, "travels" to towns where she gets drunk and picks up men. "I don't want to have any secrets from you," James says, in one of the series' more significant lines. "It's the secrets that people keep that destroy any chance they have of happiness."

Back at Renault's apartment, Cooper finds two clues that remind him of his dream. They find a copy of *Flesh World,* which features a picture of Laura Palmer, scantily clad, against. . . *red drapes.* Taped to the inside of a cabinet door, Cooper sees a picture of Jacques' cabin, which also has. . .*red drapes.*

Donna, James, and Madeleine meet at the Double R Diner. Donna looks nervous as James bounces up to get a drink for Maddy. Madeleine's comments are strangely self-contradictory; she tells them that she had a feeling on the day before Laura died that her cousin was in trouble. "I always felt close to her," she explains. But in the next breath, she says "I didn't really know Laura that well, but I feel like I do." James and Donna don't seem to notice the contradiction. . . but the astute viewer will doubtless notice they echo Laura's words in Agent Cooper's dream: "I feel like I know her, but sometimes my arms bend back." Madeleine agrees to look for a secret hiding place Laura had at home. Unbeknownst to them, Norma's husband Hank, returned from prison, was in the booth right behind them.

Major and Mrs. Briggs take Bobby to Dr. Jacoby for family counseling – once again, the impossibly stiff Briggs is trying to get Bobby to "open up." Alone with Bobby, Jacoby grills him about his relationship with Laura. "What happened the first time that you and Laura made love?" he demands. "Bobby, did you cry? And then what did Laura do, did she laugh at you?" Bobby's crestfallen expression suggests that Jacoby has hit the mark – and Jacoby's intensity suggests the same thing has probably happened to him. "Laura wanted to die," Bobby sobs. "Every time she tried to make the world a better place, something terrible came up inside her and pulled her back down into hell and took her deeper and deeper into the blackest nightmare. And every time, it got harder to go back up to the light."

"Laura wanted to corrupt people," Jacoby says, "because that's how she felt about herself." Bobby admits that he, too, was corrupted. The scene is packed with emotional power, but it's also enigmatic. Why did Laura turn to kinky sex and cocaine? Laura, the most popular girl in school, the girl who helped organize the meals-on-wheels program? Could this girl have turned Bobby into a vicious punk?

Cooper, Truman, Hawk, and Dr. Hayward tramp through the forest on their way to Jacques' cabin. In transit, they stop at the cabin of the Log Lady, who seems to be expecting them. "About time you got here!" she says. "Come on, then. My log does not judge!" She serves them tea and sugar cookies, and we learn that the Log Lady's husband was killed in a fire a day after their wedding. Doc Hayward says to her, "The wood holds many spirits, doesn't it?" Could he be talking about the evil in the woods?

Then, Agent Cooper is allowed to ask the Log what it saw on the night of Laura's death. The Log Lady interprets for the observant piece of wood: "Dark. Laughing. The owls were flying. Many things were blocked. . .Laughing. Two men, two girls. Flashlights pass by in the woods over the bridge. The owls were near. The dark was pressing in on her. Quiet, then. Later, footsteps. One man passed by. Screams, far away. Terrible, terrible. One voice, a girl, further up, over the ridge. The owls were silent." The Log Lady's mention of owls reminds us of the owl that hooted at Donna and James the night they buried the necklace in the woods.

As they proceed to Jacques' cabin, Cooper announces that the two girls must have been Ronette and Laura, and the two men might have been Leo and Jacques. "Who was the third man?" they wonder.

When they get to Jacques' cabin, what we think is the sound track – Julee Cruise singing "The Nightingale" – turns out to be a phonograph record, which repeats and repeats. Cooper recalls his dream – "There's always music in the air." In the cabin the men discover blood, a fragment of poker chip matching the one in Laura's stomach. . .and Waldo, the mynah bird.

At the Great Northern, the Icelanders are whooping it up at their gala. A shadowy figure waits in a nearby room. For the citizens of Twin Peaks, the visitors are figures of curiosity, because they come from a land with *no trees*. "Now, let me get this straight," Pete Martell says to one of them. "Your entire country is *above* the timber line?"

Catherine takes Ben aside and, as Audrey spies on them, confronts him with the poker chip he dropped. "Jerry gave me that," Ben says. Catherine slaps him three times, and then they fall into a passionate embrace. "Let's burn the mill," she sighs. "Let's do it tonight!" Ben tells her he'll give Josie one more chance to sell.

Back out at the bash, Jerry is trying to make an announcement when big-band music bursts out of nowhere. Leland Palmer freaks out – he starts dancing as he did with Laura's photograph. Catherine tries to conceal his madness from the Icelanders by dancing with him, improvising movements from Leland's agonized gestures. Soon, everybody is on the dance floor, crouching and clutching their foreheads, just like Leland. The scene is funny, but also deeply terrible; Audrey hides in a corner, watching and crying.

Ben moves into another room, and we see that the shadowy figure is – Josie Packard!

She has brought the duplicate ledger from the hiding place Ben described. "Then we proceed," Ben says. "Tomorrow night."

In front of the Johnsons' house, Hank Jennings jumps Leo. "I told you to mind the store, Leo, not open your own franchise," he hisses as he beats up on the trucker. Leo, in a murderous rage, goes into the house and menaces Shelly, who pulls a gun and shoots him. Leo runs into the night, snarling like an animal.

Agent Cooper returns to his room at the Great Northern, to discover Audrey in his bed.

Episode Seven

What is the controlled, obsessive Cooper going to do about Audrey? Although he's struggling to restrain himself, he tells Audrey they should just be friends. "When a man joins the Bureau, he takes an oath to uphold certain values – values that he's sworn to live by," Cooper explains. "This is wrong, Audrey; we both know it." He urges her to tell him her problems. "Secrets," he says, "are dangerous things, Audrey." "Do you have any?" she asks. "No," says Agent Cooper.

The next morning, at the station, Lucy – who's been sick lately – gets a disturbing call from her doctor. Truman and Dr. Hayward are trying to get the half-starved Waldo to speak,

71

but Cooper keeps his distance. "I don't like birds," he says – a significant admission, since the whole series, from the opening credits to Cooper's prophetic dream and the Log Lady's visions of owls, has been dominated by images of birds. At any rate, FBI forensics phones to confirm that Ronette, Laura, and Leo had been at Jacques' cabin, and a picture from a roll of film discovered at the cabin turns out to be Waldo, perched on Laura's shoulder. Cooper leaves his voice-activated microcassette recorder near Waldo's cage, hoping to catch some clues. The poker chip tells Cooper that an expedition to One-Eyed Jack's is in order, and since the casino is across the border, this is a good job for the Book House Boys.

Leo – who's not dead after all – spies on Shelly through the sight of a high-powered rifle as Bobby comes to visit. She's terrified that Leo will take revenge, but Bobby reassures her, "Leo Johnson is *history*." Leo overhears on the police radio in his truck that Waldo has been found, and he races off.

Madeleine has discovered Laura's hiding place, which contains a tape she made for Jacoby. She plays it for James and Donna. "What's up, Doc?" we hear Laura say. "I feel like I'm going to dream tonight. . .big bad ones, you know? The kind *you* like? I guess I feel I can say anything. . .all my secrets, the naked ones. . .I know you like *those,* Doc. . .

Donna, Madeleine, and James decide they must hear the tape Laura made on the night of her death.

Why is it so easy to make men like me? Maybe if it was harder. . ." Upset, James turns the recorder off. He notes that they have found all the tapes except the one dated February 23 – the night of Laura's death. They hatch a plot to get Jacoby out of his office so they can search it. "Maybe he gets a phone call – from Laura," James says.

Leaving her post at the perfume counter at Horne's, Audrey eavesdrops on the manager congratulating Audrey's coworker for her good work at One-Eyed Jack's. After they leave, Audrey finds Ronette's name in the manager's little black book. Back at the perfume counter, Audrey wheedles the phone number of the madam at One-Eyed Jack's from Jenny.

Big Ed tries to comfort Nadine, who's unable to get a patent on her drape runners.

Truman confronts Josie again about what she was doing at the Timber Falls Motel. She confesses she was taking pictures of Catherine and Benjamin. Josie says she overheard Catherine talking about a fire at the mill. "I'm not going to let that happen," she says.

At the Great Northern, Cooper – immaculately turned out in evening clothes – and Big Ed get spiffed up to go undercover as gambling oral surgeons at One-Eyed Jack's. Truman tells Cooper about Josie's suspicions concerning Ben and Catherine, but Cooper has suspicions about Josie: "How much do you know about her?" he asks Harry. "Where she's from? What she was before?"

Catherine gets a surprise visit from an insurance agent who says he needs her signature on a large life insurance policy taken out on her by Benjamin Horne. . .naming Jocelyn Packard as beneficiary! Catherine is shocked, but she's even more astounded when she finds that the secret ledger is gone from its hiding place.

Audrey, on her way to One-Eyed Jack's, sees an Oriental fellow checking into the Great Northern. Back at the station, Leo shoots Waldo the mynah. The plucky bird's blood drips on the totemistically stacked doughnuts – an apt visual metaphor for Twin Peaks, if there ever was one. Before dying, though, Waldo has left a revealing recollection on the tape recorder: "Laura? Laura?" the bird says, mimicking a female voice. "Don't go there. [Ronette Pulaski's exact words to Agent Cooper at the hospital.] Hurting me. Hurting me. . .Stop it! Stop it! Leo, no! Leo, no!"

With FBI money as gambling stakes, Cooper and Ed go to One-Eyed Jack's, using the cover names Fred and Barney. Cooper has been wired with a recording device under his shirt, and Hawk is outside with the sound equipment. Meanwhile, Maddy – dressed as Laura, complete with blonde hair – sneaks out of the Palmer house and meets James and Donna. James is shocked to see her. At the Great Northern, the Icelanders want to close the Ghostwood deal at One-Eyed Jack's. Ben calls Josie Packard, telling her to lure Catherine to the mill. Josie turns the job over to someone in the room with her. The camera pulls back to reveal who it is – Hank Jennings!

During Audrey's interview with Blackie, the madam at One-Eyed Jack's, Blackie sees through her cover story as "Hester Prynne." "Give me one good reason why I shouldn't air-mail your bottom back to civilization," Blackie demands. Wordlessly, Audrey plucks the cherry from Blackie's drink and ties the stem in a knot with her tongue. Blackie hires her on the spot.

In his office, Jacoby is watching *Invitation to Love*. "Jade, here's to old times," the character says. "Should old acquaintance be forgot." Ironically, in that moment he gets a call from Maddy, pretending to be Laura. She tells him that something is at the door waiting for him. "You're not Laura," he says. But the something at the door is a videotape. When he loads it up and plays it, he sees Madeleine (as Laura) holding a copy of that day's newspaper. He returns to the phone to talk to "Laura," who tells him to meet her at Sparkwood and 21. That, of course, is the same corner where, on the night Laura died, she jumped off James's motorbike and disappeared into the night. But the crafty Jacoby runs back to the first frame of the video, where he can see that "Laura" is standing by the gazebo in Easter Park. He recognizes the location and rushes off.

James and Donna head up to his office, and Bobby, who has been lurking in the bushes, plants a bag of cocaine in the gas tank of James's bike. As the episode closes, we see that some heavy-breathing character is spying on Laura – that is, Madeleine.

Episode Eight

The exciting season cliff-hanger was written and directed by Mark Frost. In Jacoby's office, James and Donna discover the coconut containing the heart necklace and also Laura's tape. Jacoby goes to see "Laura" at the gazebo in Easter Park, but before he can reach her, a hooded figure knocks him down, and he has a heart attack.

At One-Eyed Jack's, Cooper gets Jacques Renault to tell him about the goings-on at the cabin. Being tied up was Laura's idea, Jacques says. As Jacques leeringly describes the sexual games at the cabin, the camera moves in for an ugly close-up, and the sound track distorts. Jacques tells Cooper that Leo knocked him cold during a fight, and when he awoke, Laura, Ronette, and Leo were gone. Cooper pretends to be the secret financier of the cocaine ring and offers Jacques a private job. Through the microphone hidden on his body, Cooper sends a message to Deputy Hawk to follow Jacques when he leaves. Truman and his deputies, in police cars, surround Jacques' car, and he is arrested and charged with the murder of Laura and Ronette. Jacques grabs a gun and is prepared to shoot the sheriff, but Deputy Andy's target practice has paid off – he coolly plugs Jacques.

Later, in the hospital, Jacques reveals that taking the photos for the *Flesh World* ads was Laura's idea. He says Leo cut him with a broken whiskey bottle, and he used Leo's shirt to stanch the bleeding. He knows nothing about the abandoned railroad car.

Loving, considerate husband Leo Johnson abducts Shelly and ties her up at the Packard

Mill, which he douses with gasoline. "You broke my heart!" he says, reminding us of the broken-heart necklace.

James, Donna, and Madeleine listen to the tape from Jacoby's office. It is the same tape that Jacoby was listening to through his earphones at the close of Episode Two, but now we hear the end of it: "Remember that mystery man I told you about? Well, if I tell you his name, then you're going to be in trouble – he wouldn't be such a mystery man any more, but you might be a *history* man. A couple of times he's tried to kill me. . .But guess what – as you know, I sure got off on it. Isn't sex weird? This guy can really light my F-I-R-E. . ." And she mentions a red Corvette.

Depressed at the failure of her silent drape runners, Nadine attempts suicide. The scene, which is probably not central to the various mysteries of Twin Peaks, is nevertheless carefully directed. Nadine, dressed in a formal gown she might have worn to a high school prom, tenderly pours out the sleeping pills, and the romantic music swells, as if we were watching a love scene.

Meanwhile, Josie, distressed and on edge, gives Hank Jennings $90,000. Hank menacingly reminds her that the money is payment for his taking the rap for vehicular homicide to avoid being implicated in "a much greater crime – murder." Such a partnership, he says, is permanent – and he cuts his thumb and hers so that their blood can run together.

All this time, Catherine has been frantically looking for the lost ledger. Eventually, she enlists the help of her husband, Pete, telling him she has no one else to turn to.

Andy and Lucy share a kiss, and Lucy announces she's pregnant – is this why she's been so cold to Andy? And Bobby tips off the sheriff's office that a bag of cocaine can be found in James's motorbike. And Catherine receives an anonymous phone call telling her that what she is looking for – the missing ledger – is at the mill. Big Ed, sincerely upset, finds Nadine and calls for help.

James turns Laura's tape over to Cooper, but while he's at the station, Sheriff Truman discovers the cocaine in James's gas tank.

Bobby goes to find Shelly, but instead encounters Leo, who attacks him with an axe. In the nick of time, Hank appears and shoots Leo, who slumps on the sofa and watches the bad guy get shot on *Invitation to Love*.

Catherine shows up at the mill and finds Shelly just as Leo's fire bomb explodes. Pete races into the mill to save them.

Leland Palmer sneaks into the hospital and slowly smothers Jacques Renault, believing him to be the man who murdered his daughter. As he dies, Renault's hands flutter like the shadow of the bird in Agent Cooper's dream.

Agent Cooper looks down at the gun as it fires three shots into his chest. Will he survive?

At One-Eyed Jack's, Benjamin – who turns out to be the proprietor – signs a contract with Innar, his new Icelandic partner. He decides to celebrate by "breaking in" the new girl, who he doesn't suspect is Audrey. As we leave them for the season, Audrey, who has just had a "queen of diamonds" stitched to her midriff by a mysterious figure in a brown robe, is waiting on a four-poster bed, shocked by the image in a mirror of her father.

Dictating to Diane that what he wants is some quality sack time, Agent Cooper returns to his room. Another note is under his door, and he gets a late-night phone call. But he doesn't have time to deal with either, because just then a knock comes on the door. As Cooper opens the door, he is shot three times in the chest by a mysterious assailant.

Unanswered Questions

Whew! Confused? You're not alone. Although many fans expected the final episode of the first season to solve many mysteries – and reveal the identity of the killer – it actually raises more questions than it answers.

For instance, at the end of the season, Leo Johnson seems strongly implicated in the murder of Laura Palmer. But what's all this about mysterious letters under the fingernail? How could Leo call from Butte on the night of the murder if he is indeed the killer? And what about the murder that took place a year ago?

What happened two days before the murder that frightened Laura Palmer? The autopsy showed that Laura Palmer had sex with three men in the 12 hours before her death. Who were they? Even assuming that two of them were Leo Johnson and Jacques Renault, who was the third? Is Bobby right when, at the funeral, he says, "We all killed her"? Is it a conspiracy? And who is the man Laura says Bobby killed?

What exactly was Josie Packard's deal with Hank Jennings? Some have reported that she paid him off for killing her husband, but Hank was jailed for vehicular homicide, and Andrew Packard was killed in a boating accident. So who was the unknown vagrant that Hank killed? And speaking of Hank, what's he going to do now that he's found out that Norma was stepping out with Big Ed?

How did Dr. Jacoby get the heart necklace? And why does he wear multicolored glasses? A hint: colored lenses are sometimes used to help dyslexia patients. Dyslexia would be a tough disorder to have in a mystery where letters make up so many important clues.

What's the meaning of the cryptic clue, "Fire walk with me"?

Just how close *was* Leland Palmer to his daughter?

What *is* Agent Cooper's favorite gum, and what in the dickens does it have to do with a murder investigation?

Who is Madeleine? Is she really Laura Palmer, who killed her cousin and now masquerades as Madeleine to avoid detection? If so, why wasn't this discovered by the forensic scientist, Albert of the winning personality? Or did the two swap identities long before the murder? This theory would explain why Laura seemed so good and wholesome to some people and so evil and twisted to others. But in that case, which one of them is dead?

Who was the dark figure lurking in the forest when Bobby met Leo to buy cocaine? Who was the masked man who beat up Dr. Jacoby at Easter Park? Who is the mysterious Oriental who was going into his room at the Great Northern just as Audrey was going out?

Is Ronette Pulaski still in a coma? Will Nadine Hurley survive? Who is the long-haired man? What really went on in the cabin in the woods? Who shot Agent Cooper? And, by the way – who killed Laura Palmer?

Some Clues You Might Have Missed

The synopsis in this chapter can't begin to describe all the tantalizing and strange details in *Twin Peaks* that may have some hidden meaning – or may not. For instance, many fans have noted the plot similarities between *Twin Peaks* and the 1944 movie *Laura,* in which Gene Tierney stars as an apparent murder victim who turns out to be alive after all. In the movie, the character Laura is stalked by a man named Waldo Lydecker. In *Twin Peaks,* the incriminating bird who is in love with Laura Palmer is named Waldo, and he is discovered to be a patient at the office of a veterinarian named Lydecker.

Columnist Howard Rosenberg thinks that more clues can be found in the Alfred Hitchcock movie *Vertigo*. In this film, a police detective (Jimmy Stewart) falls in love with a blonde he's tailing – named Madeleine – who appears to commit suicide. She turns up later in the film disguised as another woman.

There are plenty of juicy clues within the series itself. For instance, when Deputy Andy breaks down in tears at the sight of Laura's corpse, Truman mutters, "Same thing as last year at Mr. Blodgett's barn." What happened at the barn to upset Andy, and did it have anything to do with the murder, similar to Laura's, that also occurred a year ago?

Don't forget that glimpse of plastic sheeting we see on the walls of Leo Johnson's house as he's beating up Shelly. Is it the same plastic Laura Palmer's body was found in? And Ben's brother Jerry, in one scene, gets a frozen leg of lamb from the Icelanders. The enormous leg, wrapped in plastic, is shaped just like the plastic package containing Laura's body.

Some skeptical viewers have even suspected Sheriff Truman, noting that when Pete Martell reports finding the body, he says, "She's dead," and instead of asking "Who?" Truman says, "I'll be right there." Notice, too, that Truman's name is a homophone of "true man."

The series-within-a-series, *Invitation to Love,* also holds clues. In one episode, the announcer says that the actress Selina Swift is playing the parts of both Emerald and Jade. Moments later, we're introduced to Madeleine. A hint that she and Laura are the same woman?

Many *Peaks* freaks have noticed that in the scene in which Cooper throws rocks at the milk bottle, he lists on the blackboard the names with the letter J. But the letters T and R also appear on the blackboard, unexplained.

Moreover, before Cooper flips the board over to reveal the map of Tibet, the letters are uncircled. When he flips it back around, the letters have been mysteriously circled. Actually, in the shot in which Cooper turns the map over to reveal the blackboard again, the letters are still not circled. Next is a wide shot showing Cooper and the others at the scene; after that is a shot of Truman and Andy. It's in the next shot, one of Cooper turning toward the blackboard and circling the letter J, that we see the T and the R already circled. It seems to be a minor continuity error. . .or is it a subliminal hint of the murderer's identity?

By the way, the hooded figure who sews the queen of diamonds on Audrey before her encounter with her dad at One-Eyed Jack's looks a lot like a dwarf, doesn't he?

Is the solution to Laura Palmer's murder contained in these clues? Who knows? Both Frost and Lynch are remaining tight-lipped, and the cast members say even they don't know the answer. But Mark Frost does offer fans one hint – study Agent Cooper's dream.

The European Version

One thing's for sure, the European version of *Twin Peaks,* which was released as a feature film on videocassette, is probably not the big tip-off some members of the press thought it

A version of *Twin Peaks* has been released as a 113-minute video in Europe, but this video is not yet available in the United States.

might be. The foreign video attempts to wrap up some of the loose ends of the series – including the meaning of the letter found under Laura's fingernail and the meaning of the message "Fire walk with me." It also identifies the killer as the long-haired man, Bob. But both Lynch and Frost deny that the culprit in the series is the same as the one in the European video.

Nevertheless, the European version of *Twin Peaks* is bound to be a hot collector's item for *Peaks* freaks – if they can get their hands on a copy. The video has not been released in the United States.

CHAPTER FOUR

THE MAN WHO DREAMED UP TWIN PEAKS

David Lynch's entire biography in the press kit for his most recent film, *Wild at Heart,* reads: "Eagle Scout, Missoula, Montana." But there's much more to the life of this quirky, brilliant, creative mastermind. Born January 20, 1946, in Missoula, Montana, Lynch was the son of a research scientist for the USDA who was transferred frequently. Lynch's childhood was spent first in Boise, Idaho, and Spokane, Washington – the same woodsy, bucolic settings that would reappear in *Blue Velvet* and, of course, *Twin Peaks*. Then his family moved to the South: Durham, North Carolina, and Alexandria, Virginia, where he attended high school.

Growing up, David Lynch had an almost blissfully happy childhood – something you would never expect from the tortured visions of childhood and parenthood that appear in every one of his films. But the sensitive boy did begin to realize that there was a darker reality behind the bland surroundings he grew up in. "Every once in a while, I would go to New York City to visit my grandparents and it would really freak me out," Lynch recalled to *Blitz* magazine. "I would see things in the subway. I think I started feeling fear. . .there was real fear of the unknown."

"You know little by little, just by studying science, that certain things are hidden – there are things you can't see," Lynch said in a *Rolling Stone* interview. "And your mind can begin to create many things to worry about. And then once you're exposed to fearful things, and you see that really and truly many, many, many things are wrong – and so many people are participating in strange and horrible things – you begin to worry that the peaceful, happy life could vanish or be threatened."

Lynch was indeed an Eagle Scout as a youth – he was even given the honor of seating VIPs at the inauguration of President John F. Kennedy. That's something to keep in mind when Agent Cooper worries aloud about "who pulled the trigger on JFK."

At first, Lynch was interested in being a painter, and he started attending weekend classes at the Corcoran School of Art in

Washington, D.C., with buddy Jack Fisk. After high school, both of them went to Boston Museum School. Lynch stayed a year, but he felt his fellow students weren't serious enough. He and Jack Fisk went to Europe in 1965. They planned to go for three years, but wound up staying only 15 days. "The mood wasn't right for me," Lynch told writers J. Hoberman and Jonathan Rosenbaum.

In late 1965, Lynch moved to Philadelphia to attend the Philadelphia Academy of Fine Art. Eventually, after marrying his first wife, Peggy, he bought a 12-room house in a deserted industrial area across the street from a morgue. Philadelphia was a terrifying experience for Lynch. "There was racial tension and just. . . violence and fear," he told writer Gary Indiana in a 1978 interview. Later, in the midst of publicity for his first commercially successful film, *The Elephant Man,* Lynch would recall to reporter Henry Bromell, "There was violence and hate and filth. A little girl pleading with her father to come home, and he's sitting on the curb. Guys ripping another guy out of a car while it's still moving. All kinds of scenes. It wasn't those things that did it, though. It was what they did when they sank inside of me. *Eraserhead* came out of that."

According to *Newsweek,* Lynch was fascinated by the body bags hanging outside the neighboring morgue. "The bags had a big zipper, and they'd open the zipper and shoot water into the bags with big hoses. With the zipper open and the bags sagging on the pegs, it looked like these big smiles. I called them the smiling bags of death." Lynch's continuing obsession with his nightmarish experiences in the City of Brotherly Love gives a new insight into Agent Cooper's words as he drives for the first time

David Lynch's films are, in part, an outgrowth of what he has seen in his own life.

into Twin Peaks: "As W.C. Fields would say, I'd rather be here than Philadelphia."

Lynch's first film experiments actually grew out of his study of painting. He designed a one-minute movie as a continuous loop to be shown on a sculptured screen, on which three human-shaped figures protruded. Total cost was $200. "There were lots of things moving and happening – it was a very active one-minute film," Lynch told Hoberman and Rosenbaum. In the film loop, six animated figures would begin to bloat, and their heads would burst into flames. "There would be all this wild business happening, and then they would get sick. And then it would start all over again."

The little film loop disgusted many of the viewers who saw it at its 1966 exhibit, but it did attract the attention of H. Barton Wasserman, a wealthy art patron who commissioned Lynch to do another continuous-loop film for his living room.

The Alphabet

The actual film turned out to be quite a bit different from the little art piece Wasserman had in mind. The four-minute piece, entitled *The Alphabet,* featured live action and animation and starred his wife, Peggy. Looking ghastly in white makeup, she lies on an enormous iron bed while a chorus of children chant "A, B, C. . .

A, B, C." The film then breaks into a number of animated scenes, including one in which a capital letter A gives birth to two lowercase a's, which start screaming wildly (Lynch used the sound of his own daughter, Jennifer, born in April 1968).

In another animated sequence, a surreal portrait begins to sprout body parts and a head snakes up on the end of a long stem from a bed in a bare room. At the film's close, we see Peggy again, covered with dots and striking some awkward poses, while the kids on the sound track sing "The Alphabet Song."

The Grandmother

Critical reaction to *The Alphabet* was confused to say the least, but the film generated enough interest to win Lynch a production grant from the prestigious American Film Institute. The film that grew out of this financial support – *The Grandmother* – was a color work in 16-millimeter film. Again, it combined live action with animated sequences. *The Grandmother* is about a little boy whose parents abuse him mercilessly for wetting his bed. The boy throws buckets of dirt and water on his pillow, and eventually a monstrous vegetable sprouts and gives a messy birth to a sweet grandmother character. Somehow, the boy's relationship with the grandmother he's produced makes him happy, despite continued abuse from his parents. But at the film's end, he's unable to stop the grandmother from whistling herself to death.

A visually shocking film, *The Grandmother* won prizes at film festivals in Atlanta, Belleview, San Francisco, and Oberhausen, West Germany. The critical acclaim was enough to secure more AFI funding for Lynch and to get him out of Philadelphia. Lynch moved to southern California and began work on *Eraserhead*.

Eraserhead

Eraserhead was a breakthrough movie for Lynch, the film that propelled him to international attention – although not all the attention was favorable (a review for *Variety* called the film "a sickening bad-taste exercise... Commercial potential for the nonsensical b&w feature is minimal.") Lasting just 90 minutes, *Eraserhead* took Lynch five excruciating years to complete.

Most of the film was shot at night, on crude soundstages built by Lynch and his small crew of five or six people in the stables behind the AFI mansion. Apart from the industrial exteriors shot in downtown Los Angeles, *Eraserhead* was filmed entirely in a deserted Beverly Hills garage, generally between one o'clock in the morning and dawn. The production, which was delayed every time Lynch ran out of money and had to seek more funding, dragged on interminably. Lynch later admitted that it was extremely difficult to maintain the right mood and intensity on the set over such a prolonged period of time. It was also difficult to keep the cast and crew; some of them worked on *Eraserhead* for nearly three years without pay.

Eraserhead is nearly impossible to describe adequately. Although it has a plot – of sorts – many of the characters' actions and words seem to take place without any apparent motivation, and Lynch indulges in several long, surrealistic asides that stubbornly resist explanation. On the surface, at least, the film is about Henry, a confused, frightened oaf who discovers that his girlfriend, Mary X., has given birth to a monstrously deformed baby (although Mary protests, "Mother, they're not even sure it *is* a baby!"). The "family dinner" at which Mary springs this surprise is a masterpiece of comedy and terror. Both Mary and her mother repeatedly dissolve into epileptic fits while Henry sits terrified at the dinner table with the idiotically grinning Mr. X. The sequence has a weird resonance with the scene in *Twin Peaks* in which Donna Hayward invites James over for dinner with *her* parents, and the troubled biker sits nervously alone at the table with Dr. Hayward.

Mary and the "baby" – a hideous mutation with a clublike head and a tiny body wrapped tightly in gauze – move into Henry's depressing little apartment, but Mary soon abandons him. (Lynch's own daughter was born with severely clubbed feet and had to be put in casts up to her waist.) Henry's fumbling attempts to care for his ghastly little offspring are interrupted by his recurrent daydreams about the Lady in the Radiator. She is a Marilyn Monroe-like character with bulbous plaster cheeks, who appears on a stage singing "In Heaven, Everything is Fine" (a ditty composed by Lynch himself).

In a mind-blowing dream sequence, occurring immediately after Henry is seduced by his voluptuous neighbor from across the hall, we see Henry's dismembered head land on a street corner, where it is quickly grabbed by a grubby young child. The boy takes Henry's head to a secret factory, where it is used as raw material for manufacturing pencil erasers – thus the film's title. The sequence is central to the structure of *Eraserhead,* even though it has little to do with the film's "plot," and its meaning is completely obscure. Lynch himself maintains that the scene means nothing at all. "When you're a painter, you don't think on the surface, so you don't ever have to articulate these things to somebody," he told Hoberman and Rosenbaum. "They're just allowed to kinda *swim.* . .and you don't really worry about what

A scene in *Eraserhead* shows a young boy taking Henry's head to a factory to be made into pencil erasers.

they mean. It's all feelings: it feels right and you know intuitively what it's all doing, and you work from that level." Lynch says he uses the same approach to his work today.

At the end of *Eraserhead*, Henry decides to kill his mutant offspring, and – apparently – winds up getting killed himself in the process. But in a white, misty light, he's united with the Lady in the Radiator – a climax Lynch calls "a happy ending," although the effect on the audience is very unsettling.

Twin Peaks fans will get a kick out of *Eraserhead*, not only because it really established David Lynch as a feature film director, but because several residents of *Peaks* put in an appearance. First among these is, of course, Jack Nance, who plays Pete Martell in *Twin Peaks* and whose performance as Henry is filled with emotional angst and physical comedy. Although Nance got his first real film acting job in *Eraserhead* (he had had earlier bit parts in low-budget films), he nearly came to regret it. Jack had to keep his hair styled in Henry's monstrous pompadour as the film's production dragged on for years; eventually he started wearing a hat to avoid ridicule.

Nance says that the global acclaim he received for his role in *Eraserhead* really hasn't done him much good. "People don't recognize me from *Eraserhead*," he told Susan King of the *Los Angeles Times*. "They never talk about the performance, because a lot of people think that Henry was a real character that Lynch found somewhere and put into a movie."

You'll also catch a glimpse of Catherine Coulson (the Log Lady) as one of Henry's neighbors, and Charlotte Stewart (Mrs. Briggs) appears as Mary X., Henry's brain-damaged girl-friend. A bona fide cult classic, *Eraserhead* is available in most video stores, although *Peaks* freaks who wish to make this harrowing cinematic pilgrimage will need to keep a sharp eye out. *Eraserhead* defies categorization, so it may appear in nearly any section of the store – horror, comedy, drama, and even

Eraserhead's central character, Henry, is played by Jack Nance, who is Pete Martell in *Twin Peaks*.

(because some of the scenes take place in outer space) science fiction.

The Elephant Man

Soon after *Eraserhead,* Lynch was hired to direct *The Elephant Man* for Brooksfilms, the production company owned by Mel Brooks. Shot in England and starring John Hurt as the hideously disfigured John Merrick, this sensitive, haunting film shot Lynch into the Hollywood big time. It netted Lynch an Academy Award nomination for best director.

The Elephant Man gave Lynch the opportunity to explore many of the same themes he developed in his earlier works – the horrors

The Elephant Man tells the story of a hideously disfigured man who is hounded by his fellow humans.

and beauties of the body, the longing for spiritual fulfillment, and, of course, the importance of dreams. All these motives centered around the character of Merrick, a figure not so unlike Henry in *Eraserhead* – an alienated freak with a heart of gold.

Filming in the U.K., Lynch for the first time had access to some of the top actors in motion pictures – Anthony Hopkins, John Gielgud, and Anne Bancroft, to name a few. Perhaps because of this lineup, Lynch used few of the "family" of actors that appear in so many of his other films; *The Elephant Man* is, for instance, the only Lynch film in which Jack Nance does not appear. The film did give Lynch the opportunity to work with veteran British character actor Freddie Jones, who plays Merrick's evil "partner." Lynch would use Jones again in *Dune* and *Wild at Heart*.

Dune

The success of *The Elephant Man* convinced movie mogul Dino De Laurentiis to offer Lynch the chance to direct *Dune*. The big-budget, sprawling sci-fi epic is based on Frank Herbert's incredibly complex classic novel about the interstellar struggles of two powerful royal families and the rise of a messiah who transforms the face of a planet. Lynch himself appears in an uncredited role in the film, as a

100

worried spice miner at a site that's about to be eaten by a sand worm.

According to Raffaella De Laurentiis, Lynch was uncompromising on the set. *Blitz* magazine reported that when a scene called for Duke Leto to blow smoke into an enemy's face, Lynch insisted the smoke be yellow, despite the fact that such smoke is extremely toxic. "Can I ask the actor to drill a hole in his cheek with just a little tube coming out of it?" De Laurentiis remembers Lynch asking. "Please, I would have done it to myself."

Unfortunately, *Dune* proved to be a critical disaster and a box-office flop. Lynch had tried

Kyle MacLachlan (right), who is Agent Cooper in *Twin Peaks,* was Paul Atreides in *Dune.* Francesca Annis (left) played his mother.

to cram too much of the monumental novel into a single film, and the results confused many viewers. Those who weren't lost by the labyrinthine plot were grossed out by some of the special effects, which included loving close-ups of boils being lanced and people being killed by having little tabs on their chests ripped out.

New Yorker critic Pauline Kael was among the kindest when she wrote of *Dune*: "Lynch doesn't bring a fresh conception to the material; he doesn't make the story his own. Rather, he tries to apply his talents to Herbert's conception. He doesn't conquer this Goliath – he submits to it, as if he thought there was something to be learned of it." Leonard Maltin was more typical of the critics who howled at the film: "You know you're in trouble when the film's opening narration. . .is completely incomprehensible!"

"The experience taught me a lesson," Lynch later told *Blitz* magazine. "I would rather not make a film than make one where I don't have final cut." And he told *Newsweek,* "That was a dark time for me. Boy oh boy, I'll tell you."

On the brighter side – at least for *Twin Peaks* fans – *Dune* introduced Kyle MacLachlan as Paul Atreides, who becomes the messiah who leads the planet Arakkis to freedom. Other *Peaks* regulars who show up in *Dune* include Jack Nance as the quaking assistant to the evil

Baron Harkkonen, and Everett McGill (Big Ed Hurley) as the leader of the Fremen warriors.

And, in a funny sort of way, *Dune* has many things in common with *Twin Peaks* besides the cast. In both, a huge collection of characters carry on their complicated plots and love affairs. And in both, dreams and prophecies seem more important than any details in the plot.

Blue Velvet

After *Dune* crashed in flames, one might have expected De Laurentiis to part company with Lynch. Instead, the producer gave Lynch a free hand in a *small*-budget picture. The result was *Blue Velvet,* unquestionably one of the most important films of the 1980s.

Described by Lynch as "The Hardy Boys go to Hell," *Blue Velvet* is the story of Jeffrey Beaumont (brilliantly played by Kyle MacLachlan), a clean-cut kid from the sleepy Northwest logging town of Lumberton. When Jeffrey discovers a severed ear in a deserted field, he and his squeaky clean girlfriend (played by Laura Dern) are plunged into a hidden world of violence, sexual perversion, and corruption.

Featuring a haunting score by Angelo Badalamenti, the disturbing mystery story was an unqualified hit with critics. Pauline Kael wrote after its premiere, "Maybe I'm sick but I want to see it again."

Blue Velvet also stars Isabella Rossellini, with whom Lynch is currently romantically involved (he has been divorced twice). Their initial meeting at a party was awkward. According to *Blitz* magazine, Lynch told her, "You look strangely familiar. You could be Ingrid Bergman's daughter."

"You idiot," a friend replied, "she *is* Ingrid Bergman's daughter!"

Rossellini plays Dorothy, a mediocre chanteuse whose child is kidnapped by the evil Frank (Dennis Hopper), a nitrous-oxide-snorting drug dealer who subjects her to sadistic, fetishistic sex. The scenes in which Frank is sexually abusing and controlling Dorothy are riveting and horrifying, but Lynch's off-camera reaction during the filming of these scenes was – uncontrollable laughter. "It was hysterically funny to me," Lynch told *Rolling Stone*. "Frank was completely obsessed. He was like a dog in a chocolate store...It has something to do with the fact that it was so horrible and so frightening and so intense and violent, that there was also this layer of humor."

Peaks freaks will find a lot to love in *Blue Velvet*. It has all the elements that make *Twin Peaks* so riveting: a mysterious murder, a drug ring involving some of the town's most respected citizens, violence, and cultic sex. Visually it bears a strong similarity to *Peaks*; many of Jeffrey's dream images are nearly

Kyle MacLachlan, who played Jeffrey Beaumont, with Isabella Rossellini in *Blue Velvet*.

identical to Agent Cooper's, and the slow-motion, too-pretty establishing shots of Lumberton look just like the sequence of images that run under the opening credits of *Twin Peaks*. It even has Jack Nance, in a small role as one of Frank's snickering minions. It, too, is available at video stores.

Wild at Heart

Many critics have commented on *The Wizard of Oz* references in Lynch's latest film, *Wild at Heart*. But actually, the links between the two movies are so overt that you could call the film a *remake* of *The Wizard of Oz* – perhaps the only kind of remake possible in post-nuclear, post-Reagan America.

Lynch adapted the screenplay from Barry Gifford's novel. The film follows Sailor (Nicolas Cage) and Lula (Laura Dern), two passionate young lovers fleeing from killers hired by Lula's mother, who fears that Sailor will tell her daughter of her mother's complicity in her father's death. In between bouts of wild and goofy pillow talk, their journey is punctuated by all manner of freaks, omens, and danger. Lynch seems to be suggesting that in today's world, the Wicked Witch is just as likely to come after you with a sawed-off shotgun as a broomstick.

David Lynch (right) directing Nicolas Cage in the acclaimed film *Wild at Heart*.

"I think that Sailor and Lula are trying to live *properly,*" Lynch told *Rolling Stone.* "They're struggling in darkness and confusion, like everybody else. Sailor has this tender side. . .He sings and deals with emotion, but at the same time, a definite coolness and rebellious thing is running side by side it. The idea that there's some room for love in a really cool world is really interesting to me."

Nicolas Cage said of Lynch in *Blitz* magazine, "I think that is part of his gift – to free his actors and get them to places they wouldn't normally go to. He has a playful set that is very open and relaxed. He likes to give you surprises and you react off them."

"The characters in this film are the kind of strange souls that are more real in our dreams or nightmares than in reality," says Isabella Rossellini. "They are people that one just imagines are out there but hasn't encountered before."

Certainly the critical reaction has been rewarding; *Wild at Heart* won Lynch a prestigious Palm d'Or at the Cannes Film Festival, boosting his international stature and winning even more attention for *Twin Peaks.*

Part of the fun for *Twin Peaks* fans is spotting all the cast members of the television show who make an appearance in the film. There's Grace Zabriskie, who plays Mrs. Palmer on *Twin Peaks* and the insane, crippled voodoo murderer Juana in *Wild at Heart*. Sherilyn Fenn (Audrey Horne) has a brief walk-on – or should we call it a die-on? – as a girl killed in a car accident. Jack Nance plays O.O. Spool, a resident of Big Tuna, Texas, who keeps raving about his dog. And even Laura Palmer – Sheryl Lee – shows up in the film's climax as the Good Witch, complete with crown, wand, and floating bubble.

Videos, Commercials, and Other Projects

Lynch is no stranger to television; his first small-screen program was titled *The Cowboy and the Frenchman,* an odd comedy/drama that has aired only in France. Along with *Twin Peaks,* Lynch and Frost will have another television offering for the 1990–91 season: a documentary series for the Fox network entitled *American Chronicles*. Episodes will focus on such archetypical American events as the Mardi Gras festival in New Orleans, the Miss Texas beauty pageant, and a high school reunion in Elmhurst, Illinois. The series is scheduled to air on Saturday evenings, in the half-hour time slot just before *Twin Peaks* airs on ABC. "Fox, fortunately for us, goes off the air at 10," Frost joked to the *Los Angeles Times*. "I haven't yet persuaded them to put a little subliminal message about switching to your local ABC affiliate. But I'm working on it."

Lynch and Frost are also considering the notion of developing a comedy series and a miniseries or two.

Lynch recently directed a series of ads for Calvin Klein's Obsession perfume. Done in Lynch's typically languid style, the ads recreate scenes from famous novels, and Lynch uses many of the actors from *Twin Peaks*. "I've also done a public service announcement for New York City on trash and rats," Lynch told *Entertainment Weekly*. "It's in black and white. And I had a really good time doing *that*."

But fears that Lynch is going for a quick buck doing lots of commercials are unfounded. "He's not actively looking to do commercials," Lynch's agent, Tony Kranz, told *Back Stage* magazine. And a spokeswoman for the advertising agency that handled the public service announcement on rats added, "Basically, I can't see this guy selling toilet paper."

Lynch's *Industrial Symphony No. 1,* a multimedia piece written with the composer Angelo Badalamenti and first performed in 1989 at the Brooklyn Academy of Music, has also been released on videotape.

In addition to filmmaking, producing, directing, writing, and composing, Lynch finds time to dabble in cartooning. His weekly comic strip, "The Angriest Dog in the World," appears in *The L.A. Reader* and is syndicated nationally. "It is four panels that never change," Lynch told

Blitz, "three in the day and one at nighttime, featuring a dog that is bound so tightly with anger that it approaches the state of rigor mortis. The only changes in the strip are the dialogues in the last frame, which come from the outer world. The humor in the strip is based on sickness, the sickness of other people's pitiful state. But it thrills me."

The Director Comments

Lynch admits he is trying to bring to *Twin Peaks* some of the dreamy surrealism he creates so effectively on the motion picture screen. "These shows should cast a spell," he said in a *Newsweek* interview. "It's sort of a nutty thing, but I feel a lot of enjoyment watching the show. It pulls me into this other world that I don't know about."

At first, Lynch was puzzled by the phenomenal success of *Twin Peaks.* He told *US* magazine: "I didn't know about all these numbers or how fast they'd come in. All I know was that the pilot was on the air. And I didn't really understand what the numbers meant when they did come in. People kept having to explain things to me: 'David, you just don't understand how good this is.' They went out of their way to convince me that it was, you know, very good, and that something, you know, *strange* had happened."

Nevertheless, Lynch has picked up fast on the ratings game. "I never thought I'd be watching numbers like I am," he told *Newsweek,* "but I love the cast, I love the place of Twin Peaks and the coffee and doughnuts. I don't want to say goodbye to them, so I'm sitting on the edge of my seat waiting to see what will happen."

While many expected that Lynch might fare poorly with the structural constraints of commercial television, he says he enjoys directing for TV. "You do have these breaks every 11 minutes or so," he told *Entertainment Weekly,* "and so if you can make the scenes work and put a couple together, you hit a commercial and then it's a whole new ball game when you come back. You do find yourself thinking in terms of making these little 11-minute movies, and it's kinda neat." Lynch has even joked that he's considering making a feature film that would be interrupted at regular intervals by theater staff selling doughnuts.

"I don't know where it will go in films from now on, but I love TV because you have the time to discover so many things about so many people," Lynch told *The New York Times*.

Lynch certainly has been a busy guy, but he downplays rumors that his heavy schedule will distract him from involvement with *Twin Peaks*. "I really love the show and I want to be involved," he told *US*. "I'll be right in there."

CHAPTER FIVE

BEHIND THE CAMERA
AT TWIN PEAKS

Mark Frost — The Other Guy

at Twin Peaks

Mark Frost, the *Hill Street Blues* veteran and one half of Lynch/Frost Productions, brings just as much of his personal background to the series as Lynch does. As a child, Frost spent his summers at his family's vacation home, located in Taborton in upstate New York. There, he became fascinated with the town's secrets, which included hidden affairs, political intrigues, and stories about the ghosts of murdered girls haunting the forests. "But it was all so hard to pin down because they were always just things that you would hear, and you never, never asked questions," Frost recalled to the *Los Angeles Times*.

Frost came to Hollywood in 1976, where he joined Steven Bochco on the writing staff of *The Six Million Dollar Man*. He left that show after a year to work as a PBS documentary producer and to write plays for the Guthrie Theater in Minneapolis. It was several years before he returned to L.A., once again at the invitation of Steven Bochco, to write for *Hill Street Blues*.

When *Hill Street* was finally taken off the air, after six years, Frost wrote the screenplay for the film *The Believers,* directed by John Schlesinger. He teamed up with David Lynch in 1986. The duo wrote two feature screenplays, entitled *Goddess* and *One Saliva Bubble,* neither of which attracted studio backing. *Twin Peaks* was the first commercial success for what came to be called Lynch/Frost Productions.

"The germ of *Twin Peaks,*" Frost told the *Seattle Weekly,* "came out of David and I just talking about a town, a city in the Northwest full of mysteries, secret relationships, a sort of *film noir* undertone. . .That led to the idea of starting with the discovery of a body, a mysterious crime that would get the show off the ground, serve as a spinal column for the series. That in turn led us to topography, a map of the town, and that gave way to a history of the town that ended up going back over 100 years. And that suggested what kind of people lived there now and their interrelations, the

Much of the imaginary town of Twin Peaks is really in Snoqualmie, Washington. Here is the railroad bridge Ronette walked across.

way their pasts are connected, with the town's and each other's."

"One of the reasons our partnership is relatively free of contention is that we have a shared perception about what the world is, what reality is, what life is," Frost told *The New York Times*. "There is a design behind the world that we are living in, which is veiled to most of us most of the time, but every once in a while you catch a glimpse of it. To David Lynch, any film or television show should be life casting a shadow."

The production firm that participates in *Twin Peaks,* Propaganda Films, is one of the hottest in Hollywood. The company was founded by Steve Golin and Sigurjon Sighvatsson. (Sighvatsson is a native of Iceland and the target of some gentle humor by Lynch and Frost, who show the Icelanders in *Twin Peaks* as a pack of loud-mouthed party lunatics.) Propaganda Films formed its reputation producing music videos for acts such as Madonna, Sting, Paula Abdul, and Guns N' Roses. The company played a major role in producing Lynch's latest film, *Wild at Heart*.

Goings-on Behind the Camera

Often, what's going on behind the camera during filmings of *Twin Peaks* is just as fascinating – and bizarre – as what's up front. On the set, Lynch is known for maintaining an open, playful atmosphere. In one shooting session for *Twin Peaks,* reporter Larry Rohter discovered Lynch sporting a hunting cap and waxing enthusiastic over a jailhouse scene. Meanwhile, a crew member began to blow soap bubbles, and Lynch stopped everything to watch, a broad smile on his face.

"Textures are very important to him," Catherine Coulson, who plays the Log Lady, told *The New York Times*. "He'll stop and examine a little bundle of ants crowding on top of a piece of muffin and say, 'Look at that, isn't that a beautiful thing,' and really mean it."

"Here's how he'll work," Jack Nance told writer Susan King. "You have a scene, and there's a moment when the cameras are rolling, but the director hasn't called 'action.' You are still yourself, you are the actor, but you are not committed to the scene yet. That's the moment David will use the most. He will talk to you and give you little things to say. I don't know how much in the pilot, if any, was written. We would be waiting to go, and he would come up and say, 'Say, Wrapped in plastic,' and the cameras would be rolling. He would give you this great stuff to say. It's real neat."

Lynch thinks about his directing carefully, but he maintains a playful atmosphere on the set.

The "Real" Twin Peaks

The exteriors for *Twin Peaks* were filmed in Snoqualmie, Washington, an actual logging town about 25 miles east of Seattle. Other exteriors are shot in North Bend and Fall City, just minutes from Snoqualmie on Washington Highways 202 and 203.

At first, the townsfolk of Snoqualmie welcomed all the attention they received when Lynch selected the area as the setting for the series. But many Snoqualmites are worried that America's getting the wrong idea about their little town. They were downright outraged over an article that appeared in the supermarket tabloid *Star* claiming that the woods in the area are crawling with members of a satanic cult and that "scores" of people have leaped to their deaths over Snoqualmie Falls. When not sacrificing chickens or committing suicide, the local loggers go at each other with guns and chain saws – according to the *Star*.

"Nobody is happy with the *Star* article," Snoqualmie mayor Jeanne Hansen told the *Los Angeles Times*. Even so, some of the town's residents have reacted in good humor; nearby Hangchow Restaurant has added a new coat of arms, featuring crossed chain saws, and a sign outside Big Edd's Dine In/Drive Thru Restaurant reads, "Please Check Your Chain Saw Before Entering."

And while the stories of satanic cults may be overblown, the town was temporarily home to one famous mass murderer – serial sex killer Ted Bundy, who was executed in 1989 in Florida.

The exterior of the Great Northern, the nerve center of Benjamin Horne's evil empire, is actually the Salish Lodge, a popular resort near Snoqualmie. The lavish, modern country inn is popular for its breakfasts – Agent Cooper would identify with that – and for its romantic setting near Snoqualmie Falls. The crew of *Twin Peaks* spent five days at the Salish Lodge in the fall of 1989, shooting exteriors of the lodge and location shots of the 268-foot falls. The hubbub caused by the filming created a few inconveniences for the staff; because the sign in front was covered during the exterior filming, several patrons drove right on by.

The Salish Lodge provides the exterior for the Great Northern, but most of the interiors are shot at the Kiana Lodge on Bainbridge Island in Puget Sound. The Kiana also provides settings for the Blue Lake Lodge, where Pete and Catherine Martell and Josie Packard live.

Nearby the Salish Lodge, in North Bend, is the Mar T Cafe, which is the exterior of Norma Jennings's Double R Diner. The setting is pure *Twin Peaks,* and the cherry pie is delicious. Lynch created the sign for the Double R Diner by placing two orange neon Rs above the Mar

The Salish Lodge at the top of Snoqualmie Falls forms the setting for the Great Northern in Twin Peaks.

T's cafe sign. "RR" is, of course, the common abbreviation for railroad, but doesn't *Twin Peaks* also feature two Roberts – Bobby Briggs and Bob, the long-haired man?

The Sheriff's Department is portrayed by a Weyerhauser administration building. The Road House is right on the junction of Highways 202 and 203 in Fall City, and it's really called the Colonial Inn.

And how's this for a weird coincidence – there is not just one pair of mountains called Twin Peaks near Snoqualmie, there are actually *two* pair! One is 15 miles north of North Bend, and it can be glimpsed in some of the exterior shots in the series. But another set of Twin Peaks is located 20 miles farther northeast in the Snoqualmie National Forest, near the village of Silverton.

CHAPTER SIX

"THERE'S ALWAYS MUSIC IN THE AIR"

"I love this music," Audrey Horne tells Donna as she listens to some ethereal, jazzy piece emanating from the jukebox at the Double R Diner. "Isn't it too dreamy?"

Dreamy is the word for it, all right. In *Twin Peaks,* as in most of David Lynch's films, music is so important that it's almost a character in itself. The series sound track, which at times sounds like a soap-opera score on Percodan and at other times sounds more like bebop from Venus, crests at odd times in the series – at the discovery of Laura Palmer's corpse, for instance. Throughout the series, the recurring themes are effectively used to underscore emotional impact, reinforcing Lynch's vision of romance and evil.

The musical genius behind *Twin Peaks* is Angelo Badalamenti, an award-winning composer who also collaborated with Lynch on the scores for *Blue Velvet, Wild at Heart,* and *Industrial Symphony No. 1,* a multimedia piece that premiered on stage in November 1989 and was released on video in the fall of 1990. Badalamenti has also written the scores for *Cousins, Tough Guys Don't Dance, Wait Until Spring,* and *National Lampoon's Christmas Vacation.*

Angelo Badalamenti, the creator of the eerie, hypnotic *Twin Peaks* music, has collaborated with Lynch on other projects.

In addition, Badalamenti has written scores for commercials, including David Lynch's ads for Obsession perfume. He has occasionally turned his hand to arranging, producing out pieces for such pop groups as the Pet Shop Boys.

Angelo Badalamenti worked with Lynch in the fall of 1989 to create the romantic, ominous music for *Twin Peaks*. After 20 minutes, he told *Entertainment Weekly,* he had produced the signature theme for the series, which he calls the "Love Theme." "You just wrote 75 percent of the score," Lynch told him excitedly. "It's the mood of the whole piece. It *is Twin Peaks*."

"David and I read each other very well in the creative world," Badalamenti said in the interview. "We can tune in to each other." According to Badalamenti, Lynch describes the mood he wants to create. Then the composer begins to improvise on one of the banks of electronic keyboards at his Manhattan studio. Lynch makes suggestions to fine-tune the piece, and the composition proceeds from there.

Julee Cruise performs the vocals for the two Lynch/Badalamenti compositions featured in *Twin Peaks,* "The Nightingale" and "Falling." She also appears as the lead singer of the group that's performing at the Road House just before the big fight breaks out. A native of Iowa, Cruise has been performing professionally from the age of 11. In Minneapolis, she performed at the Guthrie Theater and was a resident actress at the Maro Jones Children's Theater. Her stage credits include *Cabaret, Annie,* and *Little Shop of Horrors.* Lynch used her previously, to perform the song "Mysteries of Love," which features prominently in the sound track of *Blue Velvet.*

According to Cruise, she worked hard to develop the vocal style she uses in the songs and in the album Lynch and Badalamenti produced, *Floating into the Night.* "I had to stop smoking. I started running. I really changed everything," she states in the publicity material for the album. "Singing as clear as you can is a real challenge, as opposed to 'loud is better.' I had to come up with a whole new style of singing that was really apart from my other work.

"I'm extremely proud of what we've done," Cruise says of the album. "It's very hard to describe this music to people; it's somewhere between the '50s and the '90s, and it's such a white, white sound – a white angel sound."

"White angel sound" pretty accurately describes the effect achieved on the album *Floating into the Night.* The album contains ten tracks; in addition to the two songs from *Twin Peaks,* "Falling" and "The Nightingale," it includes "Mysteries of Love," which Lynch used in *Blue Velvet. Peaks* fans will want the first two, of course – as a memento of the show and because the lyrics, which can be virtually incomprehensible on the densely laden sound track of the series, are included with the liner notes. But the other seven compositions – all with lyrics written by David Lynch – are also extremely listenable and provide still further insight into the imagination of the director.

Lynch's lyrics all seem to take place in some sort of dream. They are filled with images of floating and fire and memories and are punctuated with quirky asides. "I never felt a wind/So happy and warm/That sent seven little red birds up my spine," Lynch writes in "I Remember." Some of the references are just plain impenetrable: "Shadow in my house/The man he has brown eyes/She'll never go to Hollywood," some of the lyrics from "Rockin' Back Inside My Heart," seem more like random ramblings from one of Agent Cooper's dreams than a comprehensible love song.

Backing Cruise's ghostly voice and Lynch's haunting, haunted lyrics is more arresting music by Angelo Badalamenti. *Peaks* freaks will recognize the composer's hand throughout the album; at times a zany sort of cool jazz, at other times a murky, evocative romanticism. The three artists serve up a pretty rich stew – one that may become a little annoying after repeated listening, but that you'll treasure having around for those nights when you want to create a little mystery. . .and danger.

Julee Cruise, the vocalist in the album *Floating into the Night,* also appears on-screen in *Twin Peaks.*

CHAPTER SEVEN

HOT BLACK COFFEE AND CHERRY PIE

Logjam — The *Twin Peaks* Quiz

All right, everybody – put on your thinking caps and stuff wads of cotton in your ears, because here's a little quiz to see how well you know *Twin Peaks* trivia. Some of the answers to these questions you can get just from having read this book. Others – and you *Peaks* freaks will know which ones they are – can be deduced only from watching the series. And some answers are revealed only in dreams and visions. . .

1. As Leland Palmer moans, "We've got to dance for Laura," what song is playing on the record player?
2. Who actually made the pot of coffee that Pete finds the fish in?

3. What is Agent Cooper's room number at the Great Northern?
4. What's the name of Leo Johnson's truck?
5. What, according to Agent Cooper, is the true test of any hotel?
6. What does Agent Cooper whittle during the stakeout at the Road House?
7. What restaurant does Cooper recommend when you're driving to Twin Peaks?
8. What lines the interior walls of Leo Johnson's house?
9. What's the name of the most popular television show in Twin Peaks?
10. What's the name of the park where Dr. Jacoby sees Madeleine disguised as Laura Palmer?
11. In addition to her diary, what piece of evidence found in Laura Palmer's bedroom does Cooper inspect in the first episode?
12. Cooper's and Ed's code names at One-Eyed Jack's are strangely reminiscent of the names of the stars of another famous television program. Which one?
13. What does Jerry say when Ben tells him the Norwegians have left?
14. Ben suspects the Icelanders are sniffing nitrous oxide. In what David Lynch film does nitrous oxide play a prominent role?
15. What did the one-armed man sell before he sold shoes?

Answers on page 128.

The Wit and Wisdom of Agent Cooper

"Two things that continue to trouble me – and I'm speaking here not only as an agent of the Bureau but also as a human being. What really went on between Marilyn Monroe and the Kennedys. . .and who pulled the trigger on JFK?"

"I want two eggs, fried hard. I know, it's hard on the arteries. . .just about as hard as I want those eggs."

"Twenty-four-hour room service must be one of the premier achievements of modern civilization."

"I'm a strong sender."

"In the heat of an investigative pursuit, the shortest distance between two points is not necessarily a straight line."

"I'm gonna let you in on a little secret. Every day, once a day, give yourself a present. Don't plan it, don't wait for it, just let it happen. It could be a new shirt at the men's store, a catnap in your office chair. . .or two cups of good, hot, black coffee."

ANSWERS: 1. *Pennsylvania 6-5000*. 2. Josie Packard. 3. Room 315. He dictates it on his tape to Diane. 4. "Big Pussycat." It's shown in Episode Two. 5. "That morning cup of coffee." 6. A wooden whistle. 7. The Lamplighter Inn. 8. Plastic sheeting. 9. *Invitation to Love*. 10. Easter Park (get it? Easter? As in rising from the dead?). 11. A box of chocolate bunnies. 12. *The Flintstones*. 13. "We had those Vikings by the horns!" 14. *Blue Velvet*. 15. Pharmaceuticals.